PRAISE FOR LEE McCLAIN AND *MY ALTERNATE LIFE*!

"Witty, dramatic, well paced, a page turner. Trinity stands up and lives on the page: gutsy, vulnerable, street-smart, people-smart—okay, just plain smart—a survivor with a heart."
—Nancy Springer, Edgar Award–winning author

"This is an absolutely refreshing read. McClain writes realistically about fashion, cliques, teenage sexuality and what happens when you're fifteen and desperate."

—*RT BOOKclub*

"Lee McClain has created a diamond among cubic zirconia with *My Alternate Life*. Filled with wonderful characters, both main and supporting, as well as an extremely fresh and original plot, this is sure to be a winner in the eyes of teenage readers the world over."

—Erika Sorocco, *The Community Beagle*

"*My Alternate Life* was a book that I couldn't put down. Lee McClain has mastered the art of writing a truly heartwarming story that incorporates the humor and irony of life with serious issues."

—*Romance Reviews Today*

TRYING TO BE NORMAL

"Brian!" came a familiar shrill voice. "Are you okay? Someone said you were fighting!" Mara rushed over and started examining Brian, who was of course completely unhurt.

"I'm fine," he said, twisting away from her.

"Why are you and Tim fighting?"

"He's got some bug up his rear end about Rose," Tim grumbled. "Jeez, can't a guy get a private minute with his date around here?"

Mara turned and saw me. Light dawned in her hostile, rapidly narrowing eyes. "You brought this on."

"Excuse me?"

"I know what you're trying to do."

"I'm *trying* to go out in a normal way, without anyone pressuring me or hitting my date or yelling at me."

Other books by Lee McClain:
MY ALTERNATE LIFE

MY ABNORMAL
LIFE

LEE McCLAIN

SMOOCH NEW YORK CITY

SMOOCH ®

March 2005

Published by

Dorchester Publishing Co., Inc.
200 Madison Avenue
New York, NY 10016

ISBN 0-8439-5466-3

Printed in the United States of America.

Visit us on the web at www.smoochya.com.

ACKNOWLEDGMENTS

I'd like to express my appreciation to Dr. David Droppa and Dr. Marilyn Sullivan-Cosetti, my Social Work colleagues at Seton Hill University, for helping me to understand foster care hearings and procedures. I also owe a debt to the Writing Popular Fiction community at Seton Hill, especially Nancy Alberts, Felicia Mason, and Nancy Springer, who offered ideas and encouragement at just the right time. Mike and Gracie: thank you for being proud of my writing instead of expecting good housekeeping. You're the best!

MY ABNORMAL
LIFE

Chapter One

Okay, so it was a dumb idea, convincing my re-tarded sister Danielle to hide in the back of an Ethan Allen furniture truck.

But as I hunched on the bottom porch step of a strange house in a strange town on a damp January day, it was the best escape plan I could manage.

Nothing had gone right since Social Services had stuck their collective noses into our lives one week ago. This was the worst yet. I was waiting outside because I couldn't stand to watch Dani get settled in her new home.

Without me.

That was when I saw the truck and heard the furniture movers complaining that their next stop was all the way in the middle of Pittsburgh.

Where Dani, Mom, and I lived. Hmmmm.

The seed of my big idea planted itself in my

mind, and I stood up and strolled closer to the truck, keeping my eyes down, making myself as invisible as I could.

Behind me, the door to Dani's new home burst open and a guy my age slammed out onto the front porch. "Don't pay any attention to what I want," he yelled. "You never do!"

The door closed behind him.

Even I, Miss Zero Experience, could see that the boy was sexy. He had broad, powerful shoulders and dark brown hair that curled over the sheepskin collar of his coat.

And, oh my gosh, his eyes. I mean, I have brown eyes, but like everything else about me, they're ordinary and forgettable.

This boy's brown eyes looked like melted chocolate. They drooped down at the outside corners, like he was just a little bit sleepy. But there was nothing sleepy about the athletic way he took the porch steps in one leap and strode down the walk.

I hadn't been this close to a good-looking boy in forever. Mostly I'd just watched them out our apartment window, or on TV. So I got a disloyal flash of, "Hey, maybe it won't be so bad in this town," as I watched him walk toward me.

My prince, coming to my rescue?

"Why can't you people solve your own problems?" he yelled in my direction.

My warm, fuzzy feeling evaporated. "Us people? Excuse me?" I marched toward him, ready to fight. I may be short but I'm strong.

His cell phone rang and he turned away like I wasn't even there. "Yeah?" he said into it. "Oh, just another Little Orphan Annie my folks have taken in. I was supposed to be home to, quote, make her feel welcome, but I'm bailin'."

"We're not orphans," I protested to his broad back.

Just at that moment, Dani came out onto the porch. She was crying with her mouth wide open, loud wails that reached into my chest and pierced my heart.

I ran up the steps and wrapped my arms around her. "Hey, it's okay," I said, even though it wasn't. I stroked her tangled, light brown hair and patted her bony back.

Her wails slowed, then stopped. "I not stay here," she said, her voice shaky. "I stay *you.*"

My point exactly. I looked up at the screen door of the house, where our social worker Fred and the new foster mom stood watching.

"You can visit each other," Fred said.

"After she has a few days to settle in." The foster mom crossed her arms over her chest. Her chin was pointy like a witch's. "Rose, she needs to hear from you that it's okay for her to stay here."

"You want me to lie?" I said it quietly so that Dani, whose head was now buried in my shoulder, wouldn't hear.

The foster mom's lips tightened. "Say your goodbyes," she said. "Fred, we need to nail down some details."

The two of them disappeared back into the house.

Dani clung to me. "I stay *you*," she repeated over and over.

Her words tore at my heart, and what made it worse was that it was all my fault. If I hadn't tried to shoplift food from a new store whose owner I didn't know, the police would never have found out how Dani, Mom, and I were living.

Stupid, stupid, stupid.

It was bad enough being taken away from Mom, not to mention my apartment and my neighborhood and everything I knew. But I'd thought Dani and I could stay together. Putting us in separate homes in the same small town was the bright idea of our counselors at St. Helen's Home for Girls.

After having known us for all of one week, they'd decided I was overly responsible and prematurely adult. And they thought Dani, at eight, was too attached to me.

Well, duh. What choice did we have?

And what was so bad about being responsible and attached?

So now, just because I'd answered some questions wrong in their interviews, I couldn't stay with Dani and help her get used to a new place.

4

My grandma's words came back to me: "You're this baby's guardian angel," she'd said when Dani was born with Down syndrome. "With the good Lord's help, you have to keep her safe, whatever your mother and father do."

Well, Gram, I thought, looking up toward heaven, *you better tell the good Lord to step in quick.*

Dani wrapped herself around me like a monkey and I carried her down the porch stairs.

And there sat the truck, wide open. The back of it was half full of furniture. The delivery guys were inside the next-door neighbors' house.

"Hey, Dani," I said, "want to play a game?"

She lifted her head. "What game?"

I dug a used tissue out of my jeans pocket and wiped her nose. "See that truck?" I said. "We're gonna play hide-and-seek in it. Hold on."

I glanced back at the doorway of Dani's new foster home. Still empty. Then I scrambled up the ramp that led into the back of the truck and looked around. There were a couple of big dressers we could hide behind and some green padded blankets to pull over the top of us. Perfect!

"Hey," said a voice outside the truck.

I froze.

"Are you crazy? What're you doing?"

Slowly, I turned around.

It was Mr. Sexy. "I gotta go," he said into his cell phone, and stuffed it in the pocket of his windbreaker. "Get outta there," he said to me. "Any minute now, they're going to shut this truck and drive off. You can't play in there."

I put Dani down but kept my hands on her shoulders to soothe her. "We're not playing," I said.

He came closer, hoisting himself up to sit on the back of the truck. "My mom's gonna kill you."

"Look, just get out of here before somebody sees you," I hissed. "We're taking care of our own problems, okay? We're trying to go back home."

"You're stowing away?" He sounded the slightest bit impressed.

"It dark in here," Dani said.

"I know. We're playing cave." It was a game we played whenever the lights got turned off at home.

Dani started to cry. "I no like cave!"

I sighed. "Look," I said, kneeling down to face her. "We're going to go for a ride in this truck. A long ride, but I'll be right here with you all the time. And when it opens up again, we'll be back home."

"Are you out of your mind?" asked the boy.

"Just get out of here so nobody sees you," I snapped. "This isn't your business."

"Brian!" a woman's voice called. "Did you see where Dani and her sister went?"

I heard more people coming this way. "Off the

truck, kid," said a male voice. "We're heading out."

I put my hands together to pantomime a prayer to the kid. And then I had to focus on Dani. "Come on, down here," I whispered, and pulled her behind the biggest dresser with me. "Look, we'll put this blanket over us. Be real quiet!"

A big sliding door came down, blocking all the light from the back of the truck.

The engine rumbled to life.

Dani started crying again.

As the truck started moving, I hugged her tightly and tried to feel good about getting away. I'd always taken care of our family. Usually, though, I had a little more time to sort through alternatives and make a plan. This time I'd made a snap decision.

Sometimes being responsible sucks. Because what if you make a really big mistake?

At least we're together. I hugged Dani tighter. *And we're away from that mean foster mom.*

The truck screeched to a halt. Angry voices argued outside.

"What that man talk about?" Dani asked me.

"Sssh." I put my hand over her mouth, but gently so she wouldn't get mad. "We're playing a game, remember? We have to be really quiet."

"I no like cave!" she said, still crying a little.

The back of the truck opened with a screechy metal-on-metal sound, and light flooded in.

7

"Anybody back here?" a man's voice called.

"Well, they're hardly likely to answer you," came the foster mom's witchy voice.

Dani jumped out of my grip. "Here we are!" she crowed.

Caught!

I let my head sink down into my hands for one tiny moment. Then, slowly, I stood up and walked out into view.

Dani danced around, all happy, thinking the game was over and she'd won. The foster mom lit into the furniture guys for not checking their truck.

Fred, the social worker, glared at me. "What were you thinking?" he asked. "You could have gotten hurt or lost. And it's not just you, it's your sister in question."

I clamped my mouth shut and looked away. We would've been fine. I knew my way around my home turf and I'd been taking care of Dani for years.

But no way would a social worker believe in me. That wasn't in his job description.

My eyes landed on the foster brother, Mr. Sexy. "You told," I accused him. "You ran to Mommy and told."

He lifted his hands. "It wasn't me. I was ready to let you go."

"Yeah, right."

He nodded toward Fred. "It was that guy. He's

8

weird. It's like he could see you through the truck. He knew right away where you went."

"Maybe he just has a lot of experience with deceitful young people," said the foster mom. Apparently she'd finished with the furniture guys and was ready to turn her scolding tongue on us.

"Come on out, girls," Fred said, and Dani, little traitor that she was, ran to him. He helped her off the back of the truck.

I got down on my own—nobody was rushing to give *me* a hand—and right away the foster mom got on my case. "You endangered your sister. I had my reservations about you before, considering the shape she's in, but now I'm certain you're a bad influence."

That remark on top of everything else stunned me. All I'd done for eight years was take care of Dani. And now this stranger had the nerve to tell me I'd done a bad job?

Tears pushed at the back of my eyes and my throat started hurting.

Mr. Sexy must have noticed. "Mom, lighten up," he said.

She spun around. "You're just as bad, Brian," she snapped. "You saw them get into that truck and didn't tell me. If anything had happened, it would have been your fault. And with all your gifts, you should know better."

Brian's head dropped and he turned around. "I

don't want 'em here anyway," he muttered as he walked away.

Through my misery I wondered about his so-called gifts. What were they? Or was being born normal in a houseful of retarded kids considered a gift in itself?

"Come on," Fred said to me. "We're late. We have to get you settled in your new home, and I know your foster parents are eager to meet you."

I dreaded the thought.

"Dani, let's go get a snack," said the foster mom.

My little sister loved food. She turned and followed the woman toward the house.

" 'Bye, Dani," I called with a little crack in my voice. "See you soon."

"No contact for two weeks," said the foster mom over her shoulder, looking at Fred. "And only phone calls and supervised visits for the first couple of months. If you can arrange that, I won't report this little incident to the agency."

Two weeks? First couple of months? But there was so much I hadn't told The Witch about Dani. How to get her to take a bath. How *Sesame Street* always calmed her down. How she liked to be sung to sleep.

My chest felt empty, like someone had pulled my heart out of it. I took a step toward Dani.

Fred put his arm around me and guided me

toward his old beater of a car. "It'll be good for you girls to settle into your own homes," he said. "I know the McGraws want to get you involved in some school activities."

School activities? That was the last thing I wanted to think about.

"Great," I said, not bothering to hide my sarcasm. I was too busy trying to hide my tears.

Chapter Two

My first clue that things were going to be strange at my new home was when a cheerleader answered the door.

She looked a few years older than me, and pretty in a perky way: strawberry-blonde hair in a high ponytail, an athletic build, and just enough freckles to be cute. And she had the pom-poms to match the cheerleader outfit.

Huh?

Even old Fred raised his eyebrows.

"Oh, my gosh, Mom, Rose is finally here," she said. "Come on in! We've been dying to meet you." She waved her pom-poms around.

This foster mom, Joan, seemed to love me the moment she stepped into the hallway. She looked to be in her forties, but her short, curly hair was the same strawberry blonde as her daughter's, and she moved in the same bouncy way. And she was a hugger.

Too bad I wasn't.

I escaped as soon as I could and backed toward Fred.

"Oh, look at me," said the cheerleader. "I'm still in my cheerleader outfit. I must look so weird! But Mom was dying to see me in it. I just made the squad last week. At Penn State! That's, like, practically impossible for a freshman to do!"

"Dale!" Joan called.

A fat, jolly-looking man in a white shirt and suspenders came into the entryway. "Rose. You are very welcome," he said, shaking my hand long and hard. "This house has been way too quiet since our Michelle moved out." He patted the cheerleader's shoulder.

She snuggled in. "Oh, Dad, you always used to complain about the noise me and my friends made."

Joan shook her head with a fond smile. "Parties practically every weekend, and friends in for movies and pizza every night of the week. Our Michelle is a real social butterfly."

I cleared my throat. "Well, I'm not."

There was the tiniest little silence. You wouldn't have noticed it at my real house, but here it stood out.

It didn't last long.

14

"What do you like to do, Rose?" the father asked.

"Um . . . I like to read."

Joan clapped her hands. "I knew I did the right thing, keeping up our subscriptions to *Teen People* and *Seventeen*."

Everyone looked at me, so I guessed I was supposed to respond. I didn't know what to say though. I'd never really read magazines, just looked at the glossy pictures while waiting in line at the grocery store. With their make-up and trendy clothes the girls inside them had seemed so foreign. Part of a world I'd never experience.

"Well, do you like magazines?" Michelle finally asked.

When I had a free minute at the store, which wasn't often, I always hunted out the books with elves and swords and magic on the covers. "Um, sure, magazines are great," I said, knowing it was a lame, too-late response.

"Come on inside. Take your coats off," said the father.

"We have all kinds of things planned for you," said Joan. "We're eager to get you involved in a lot of activities, just like our Michelle was."

I shot Fred a look that said, *Get me out of here.*

"Maybe I could just help Rose carry her things to her room and have a few minutes alone with her," Fred said. "Then I really should be going. I don't want to interfere with your dinner plans."

"Oh, fine. Of course. We did invite a couple of girls over. Dale thought a family dinner would be best on the first night, but I said, if she's starting school tomorrow, she'll need to know at least a few people."

"She looks like she could use a good meal," the dad said.

"That's fine," Fred said, somehow managing to smile at Joan, usher me back in the direction the dad pointed, and pick up my duffel bag.

In my new bedroom—and I had to admit it was nice, all purples and pinks with crown molding and wallpaper and ruffles—I spun to face Fred. "I can't stay here. These people are crazy. They talk too much. And they have *activities* planned for me."

"Joan and her daughter are talkers, but remember, the daughter doesn't live here full-time," Fred said. "And the activities part is why we thought this would be a good match."

"I've never even been inside a high school," I argued. "I can't deal with activities too."

"You need to learn to live the normal life of a teenager, and the McGraws are the definition of normal."

"I need to get my family back together," I said, "not shake pom-poms like that overgrown cheerleader out there."

Fred shook his head. His eyes were gentle and sad and altogether too wise. "You're not going to be allowed to get your family together," he said, "until you've proven you can live like a normal teen."

I couldn't help it: I started to cry. "I'm *not* normal!" I sputtered out. "I probably can't ever be! Do Dani and Mom have to suffer because of that?"

Fred looked distressed. "Look, I wasn't going to tell you about this yet," he said, "but I have a way for you to keep track of Dani and your mom." He looked around the room until he saw the computer on the antique-looking desk. "Come here." He hit the Internet icon and typed in an address. "Take a look," he said.

Every once in a while I'd gotten the chance to play around with the computers at the public library. And when I was little, Gram had signed me up for a free computer class for kids. But I wasn't exactly familiar with the latest models. "What is it?" I asked.

"It's a computer game. Or rather, a special kind of Web site."

"I don't have time for games," I said, impatient.

"I think you'll like this one." He typed a few things in. "See, I'm telling it to go over to Dani's house. We can check on her this way."

"You put a nanny-cam over there?" I'd seen a

special about those on cable TV, right after our neighbor had spliced us in, but I'd never have pegged Fred as the spying type.

"No. This is a, shall we say, special sort of game. There are some other functions, too. You can discover those on your own." There was a sparkle in his eyes.

I watched as a splotchy video came into focus. There was Dani, sitting at a dinner table with The Witch, four other young kids who looked just as slow as Dani, and Mr. Sexy.

Seeing Dani made my chest hurt in a funny way. How many meals had she ever had without me? I was glad to see that she had plenty to eat, but she wasn't wearing any kind of a bib, and she was dribbling soup down her shirt.

The Witch was too busy feeding one of the other kids to notice.

It was Mr. Sexy who, in the end, reached over and wiped off Dani's chin.

And Social Services thought that family of strangers could care for Dani better than I could? "There's too many kids there," I told Fred. "They can't take good care of Dani."

"The Johnsons are well within state guidelines," Fred said in his mild, calm voice. "And they're required to have a certain number of training hours every year. They're very capable."

Anger surged in my chest but I stifled it. *Get more information*, I told myself. The more I knew, the quicker I could find a way to get our family back together. "Is there a dad in that family?" I asked Fred.

"He works long hours. He's a newspaper editor," Fred explained.

"And they just take in, um, slow foster kids?"

"They've actually adopted three of the four little kids you see there," Fred said. "The little boy in the red is their biological child, and so is the teenager."

I got a cold, hard feeling inside me. "Do they think they're going to adopt Dani?"

"She's not free for adoption at this point."

"And she won't ever be," I said. She wouldn't. No way! She belonged with me; she was part of me.

Fred didn't answer. Instead, he leaned over and tapped a few keys.

"Want to see your mom?" he asked as Dani's image faded.

I swallowed. "Sure."

But of course, there wasn't much to see. Mom was lying in bed in a semidark room, not moving. No one else was there.

Looking at Mom made my stomach swirl with love and hopelessness. I'd tried so many times to make her get up, just sit up and open her eyes and notice us. But she hardly ever did and in the past few months I'd given up. Sometimes I felt like I hated her.

The apartment was home, and I longed for it. But the way it was always dark and gloomy gave me a dark, gloomy feeling inside.

There was the saggy flowered couch where Gram used to read me stories about princesses and fairy queens. There was the window where I sat every afternoon watching kids with real lives go by. There was the kitchen where I'd spent so much time trying to dress up store-brand macaroni and cheese.

That memory jerked me to life. "Does Mom have anything to eat?" I asked. "Can we look in the cupboards?"

Fred shook his head. "The police officers who took you girls into custody were trying to set her up in a counseling program."

"Does she have to leave the house for it?" I looked away from the screen. It was too depressing to watch Mom sleep.

"Yes, I think so."

"She won't go." I bit my lip. "She'll starve in there. I've got to get back and get her some food."

Fred's hand closed on my shoulder. "Rose. You're a kid. You have no money for food."

"I have ways of doing things."

"So I've heard." He stood up. "I promise I'll send someone to check on your mother and make sure she has food," he said, "if you'll promise to try to be a normal teenager."

"You mean normal like this family?" I couldn't

keep the doubt out of my voice, even though I really wanted Fred to check on my mom.

"Well . . . how about going to school every day, and participating in at least one after-school activity?"

"I can try," I said, "but I doubt it's going to be cheerleading."

Fred laughed. "I do too," he said, and reached to do something else on the computer.

"Wait!" I grabbed his arm. "Can I look at this again? I mean, after you're gone? Can I check on them every day?"

He nodded. "The game has its twists and turns, but sure. Just type in this address, *www. ALTLIVES.com,* and play around. You can get audio instead, or a transcript. Just don't—" He broke off.

The tone of his voice made me stop in the middle of scribbling down the address. "What?"

"Just don't spend too much time on it until you've gotten a taste of real life," he said. "It could be risky."

"Risky how?" I asked. "Like getting addicted to soap operas or something?"

He shook his head and looked at me with a serious expression. "It's more than that," he said. "Remember—you have to learn to be a teenager. A normal, involved teenager with friends. Your future depends on that, not on getting obsessed with this game." He paused. "Let alone making certain decisions the game will ask of you."

"What are you talking about?" He made the game sound like a real, living thing. And while I had to admit it was weird to be able to see my family on a computer screen, I still figured it was some kind of a webcam. Just the wonders of technology, not something all woo-woo and mysterious.

"Never mind. That's far in the future." He patted my shoulder and pushed some buttons to make the screen go dark. "Come on. Let's go out and get you started on normal."

Chapter Three

My first full day of trying to be a normal teen was stressful. By lunchtime, I had a headache.

How did regular high school kids deal?

For one thing, high school was loud and smelly and dirty. Right now, for instance. When I put my elbow down on the table so I could prop up my aching head, it got stuck in the remains of a thousand other lunches. And I'd never smelled so many different kinds of greasy, steamy foods at once.

Also, it seemed like there were secret rules for everything: how to dress, how to act in class, and what to say when someone crashed into you in the hall, which happened to me fairly often that first morning.

I broke every one of those rules.

"See, those jeans are way out of style," said Kimber, the student who'd been assigned to help me find my classes and make me feel "at home."

As if that were possible.

"All the really cool girls wear tight, low-cut jeans. But you'd have no way to know that, being from a different town and all. Last year everyone wore baggy ones."

Her fashion advice made me glance at her dress. It wasn't like I had a clue or anything, but none of the other girls wore a long-sleeved, high-necked wool dress and stockings. She looked more like the teachers, and the older ones at that. Her reddish-brown hair, tied back in a lumpy bun, and her pale, unmade-up skin did nothing for her.

She rolled her eyes. "I know, I know. My parents are, like, totally conservative and religious. I was homeschooled up until last year, and they still control practically everything I do and wear." She paused. "That's why they matched you up with me, because we'd both been homeschooled."

"Well, sort of." The truth was that though Mom and I, and lately just I, had filled out the homeschooling paperwork, we'd never actually fulfilled the promises we made in it.

"Why'd you come to school?" I asked Kimber.

"I'm kind of this science genius, and I want to be a doctor, so I begged and begged and they let me come. But you want to know the truth?"

I nodded, even though Kimber's intensity was making my headache worse.

"I want to meet boys!" she crowed. "I'm nuts about them. I was going crazy never meeting anybody but a few silly church kids I've known my whole life."

"Do you, um, have a boyfriend yet?" I took a bite of pizza and then let the rest of the slice drop back onto my tray.

"Are you kidding? Dressed like this?" She shook her head, chomping on her own pizza slice and looking anything but distressed. "But you have a chance. I know your new parents. They're really cool. They'll buy you whatever you need to be in style."

"I don't care about all that," I said.

Her eyes widened. "You mean you don't care about boys? Are you gay?"

"No!" I wiped my hands on a napkin and stood up. "I just have other things besides clothes and boys on my mind."

"Oh." She looked glum for about two seconds, then brightened up. "Well, maybe you'll like the activities fair. It's next period, in the gym, and I'm supposed to take you there."

I sighed as we walked out of the noisy cafeteria. What I really wanted was a rest period, somewhere quiet where I could be alone. After spending twenty-four–seven in a small apartment with a mom who rarely spoke and a sister who talked like a two-year-old, I was exhausted living the life of a regular teenager.

I was surprised that so far my classes didn't look hard. Considering that I hadn't been to school since sixth grade, I expected it would be way over my head. But all I'd ever had to do was read. I'd gone through all the books in our apartment a million times, and whenever I could get out, I always hit the library. All the reading I'd done made history a breeze. And in English, we were starting Shakespeare's *A Midsummer Night's Dream.* I couldn't wait to tell Dani. We'd read it in Gram's old *Stories from Shakespeare* a million times.

In my other morning class, science, they'd put me on the slow track, so the teacher explained everything in boring detail. At first I'd been a little worried about the quiz coming up in two days, but he'd told us everything that would be on it and where to find the answers in the book.

No, it wasn't the classes that were going to be the problem. It was everything in between.

Like this activities fair.

"Check it out," said Kimber, leading me into the gym.

Tables were set up all around the perimeter, decorated with posters and photos advertising the highlights of each club. Music pounded beneath the sound of at least two hundred kids talking.

Some tables had crowds of kids around them, while others were nearly empty.

"What activities do you do?" I asked Kimber.

"What?" She cupped her hand to her ear.

"What activities do you do?" I shouted.

"Oh. Over here." She led me to one of the corner tables. One stocky, acne-faced girl sat behind it, reading a magazine.

"Hey, Kimber," she said.

"Hey." Kimber showed me the photos.

All the kids looked like Dani.

"You work with retarded kids?" I asked.

"We're not supposed to call them retarded," she said. "We say 'developmentally delayed.' "

"How come?"

She shrugged. "Just sounds nicer, I guess. Anyway, I help out in the special ed classrooms a couple of times a week."

"I could do that," I said. "My sister's retarded. I mean, developmentally delayed. She has Down syndrome."

"Really?" Kimber's eyes darkened and she put a hand on my arm. "I'm sorry. That must be rough."

I wasn't used to sympathy and it made me feel teary, especially since Dani wasn't under the same roof as I was anymore. To shift the focus

from me to Kimber, I asked, "Do you like working in special ed?"

"It's okay, but I mostly do this activity because my parents make me. I'd rather be on the
flag team or something. Come on, let's walk
around."

I wished I could just say I'd help out in special
ed and then get out of here. But Kimber looked
so eager. Besides, I wasn't sure that volunteer-
ing in special ed would qualify as making me
normal.

It was more like continuing my abnormal life.

We hung around the fringes of the flag team
table for a few minutes. Kimber looked long-
ingly at the photos and the cute little uniforms
on display.

"Why don't you join?" I asked.

She laughed. "You have to try out, for one
thing. And besides, my parents would never let
me wear these kinds of clothes or come to prac-
tice or football games or anything."

"Too bad."

She shrugged. "Just wait 'til I'm eighteen.
Come on, let's see what else is happening."

We wandered until we came to a table with
no kids in front of it. Behind it sat a boy half ob-
scured by the girl who perched on his lap, her
arm around him.

"Hi, Brian," Kimber said. "How's the paper?"

"Understaffed," he said through a strand of his girlfriend's hair.

At the sound of his voice, I did a double take. It was Mr. Sexy from yesterday!

Kimber pulled me forward. "This is Rose. She's new, and looking for an activity to get involved with."

Brian leaned sideways to look at me. "I believe we've met."

"Is Dani doing okay?" The question burst out before I could stop it.

"She had a rough night," he said, "but she was okay this morning."

A rough night, and I hadn't been there to help. My arms ached to hold Dani and my throat tightened around the words I should have said to comfort her.

"How do you know *her?*" asked the girlfriend, twisting on Brian's lap to glare at me. "And who's Dani?"

"Just . . . one of the kids at home," he said. A red flush crept up his neck.

"Oh, the mentally challenged ones?"

I didn't like her tone. "My sister Dani is living with Brian's parents for a little while," I said. "A *very* little while. She has Down syndrome."

"What's *that?*"

Before I could form an answer, Kimber jumped in. "It's a genetic disorder caused by an extra chromosome," she said. "It causes some physical abnormalities, like widely spaced, slanted eyes. Usually it causes mental retardation too."

Whoa! I'd lived with Dani for eight years and I couldn't have explained it like that.

Brian's girlfriend sneered and looked me up and down. "Is she slow too?"

"No need to be nasty," Kimber said. "Rose isn't slow."

"Like you'd know." The girlfriend flicked her hair and turned back to Brian. "Why are they talking to us, anyway?"

"Maybe we'd like to join this club." I lifted my chin and gave her a look every bit as baleful as her own. I might have been inexperienced with high school social life, but I was pretty sure this girl would be a jerk in any environment.

Her laugh was a high whinny, like a horse in pain. "It's not a club!" she squealed. "They thought it was a club!"

Kimber completely ignored the girl's attitude. "I know it's the paper, Mara," she said. "But Rose doesn't, and how would she? She's new, and your sign doesn't show."

Brian lifted Mara off his lap—nice biceps, I noted—and moved around to the front of the table to flip over the sign that had been face down. "No wonder we weren't getting many customers," he said. "How am I ever going to build up a decent staff if no one knows we're here?"

Mara studied her fingernails. It was pretty clear to me that she'd flipped over the sign so she could have Brian all to herself.

"You want to join?" he asked Kimber. "You could cover science."

She shook her head. "Can't. I'm not allowed to go to boys' houses, and you have some of the meetings at your house, don't you?"

"I'm so sure you're not even allowed to go to boys' houses," Mara said.

Brian grinned. "Honest, Kimber, we're not sneaking cigarettes or playing spin the bottle. They're just meetings."

She shook her head. "My parents aren't reasonable people."

It took a moment for my plan to fall into place. As soon as it did, I blurted out, "I'll join your staff."

"Sure, go for it, Rose," Kimber said in an encouraging voice.

Mara's forehead wrinkled. Obviously she was trying to think of a way to stop any girl from joining the newspaper.

I'd thought Brian might be happy to have a volunteer. Ha!

"Um, Rose," he said, "haven't you basically lived your whole life in a cave? How can you report the news?"

Mara snorted. "Raised by wolves, like that girl on *Extreme Natural*?"

Their comments hurt, but I didn't let it show.

No matter what, I was getting on the paper. That way, I'd have a great excuse to see Dani. Plus, I'd have an activity that wasn't crowded with yapping girls—thanks to Mara, who looked like a pretty ferocious gatekeeper.

And if the reruns of *Lou Grant* were accurate, I'd have reasons to call people and get rides into town, so there might be ways to check on Mom.

It was my best chance of getting our family back together.

"I went to school when I was younger," I said. "And I watched cable news whenever our neighbor could splice us in. I read a lot and I'm a good writer. What do you say?" I looked right into Brian's chocolate eyes.

He looked back for what seemed like a long time, and I felt a weird little tingle pass through my body.

"It would probably be smarter to say no," he said, and I noticed the red flush was back on his face. "But I do need reporters. So okay. You're on staff."

Chapter Four

"Three double mocha lattes, please." Joan forked over more money than I would have spent on groceries for a week. Then she turned to me, her face beaming in the mall's artificial light. "That's what Michelle and I always got during our shopping sprees."

I glanced at Kimber, but she just looked happy. "Thanks, Mrs. McGraw. I love mocha lattes."

As we walked toward a small, rickety-looking table in the center court of the mall, Kimber chattered away with my foster mom. I was glad I'd brought her. In the two weeks since I'd arrived, Joan had been bugging me about friends and school activities.

Kimber's knee-length, gray plaid skirt and penny loafers had made Joan look doubtful. Obviously it worried her that my only friend was hopelessly out of style. But now Kimber was winning Joan's affection by sharing her enthusiasm about hair, fashion, and the high school scene.

She would have made a great foster daughter for Joan.

"So what do you think about Rose writing for the newspaper?" Joan asked Kimber. "It's not very social, is it? Shouldn't Rose choose an activity where she can meet boys?"

Joan sounded more like a teenager than I did. How strange was that?

What Joan really wanted was for me to be a cheerleader like her wonderful daughter Michelle. Which shouldn't have mattered, but it did, especially since Joan would be describing my normality or lack thereof to my caseworker.

I took a sip of the latte. Yum!

Kimber came through for me. "The newspaper is a great activity, Mrs. M.," she said. "The editor is Brian Johnson, and he's really cool. Not to mention cute!" she added, jabbing me in the side.

I felt my face turn red.

Joan looked at me with concern. "Are those the Johnsons who have your sister?"

Don't go all perceptive on me now, Joan. I nodded. "But that's not why I wanted to join the paper," I lied. "I'm really into writing." I watched her face, feeling my way. "And writing about school events is a great way to learn what's going on."

"Brian's the star baseball player who quit to be newspaper editor last year," Kimber said. "Remember, there was an article on the sports page about it?"

"Really?" That surprised me. "So that's where he gets those shoulders. And biceps."

Joan was looking happier. "I guess the newspaper is okay," she said. "Now let's talk about your makeover."

"Ooh, a makeover!" Kimber scooted her chair forward.

"I don't want a makeover," I said. "I'm fine the way I am."

"Of course you're fine," Joan said soothingly, "but you want to make the most of your assets, don't you? With that hair and those baggy clothes, you'll have a hard time getting anyone to notice you."

"You are so totally lucky," Kimber said. "If my parents would pay for me to have a makeover, I would be so all over it."

"But I don't care about stuff like that." I felt like a stubborn little kid.

Joan stroked the hair back from my face. "You'll look so pretty with just a little shaping," she said.

Her affectionate gesture felt good, but she wasn't my mom. I pulled away.

Joan sighed and picked up her latte. "Come

on, let's finish these up. I made you an appointment at Hair Train. It's where Michelle always liked to go."

An hour later, as we walked into the juniors' department of Smithfield's department store, I felt lightheaded.

Maybe it was the loud pulsing music and colored lights. Maybe it was the challenge of holding in an hour's worth of giggles over my totally bizarre hairdresser and watching Joan and Kimber struggle to do the same. Maybe it was losing the weight of all that hair.

"Now just look at that," Joan said, pointing to a blue-and-orange-striped, ankle-length brown skirt. "Why would anyone wear it?"

"It looks ugly on purpose," I said.

"You'd look great in one of these tops," Kimber said, grabbing something slinky and red.

I straightened it out and held it against myself. "Sleeveless? But I'm always cold."

"So carry a sweater," Kimber said. "Boys like skin." She held a short orange dress up to herself in front of the mirror and let out a sigh.

I glanced at Joan, who was watching Kimber. "Why don't you try it on, Kimber?" she suggested.

"I don't want to get depressed. My parents would never let me wear anything this short."

Joan studied her. "You need to look more feminine," she said. "You dress like a professor, and as smart as you are, boys probably get intimidated."

"Believe me, it's not my choice," Kimber said.

I felt sorry for Kimber. Her parents cared, but they had no idea who their daughter was.

"Clothes don't have to be bare to be feminine," Joan said. She scanned the rack with an experienced eye and pulled out a pale pink dress. It had a swishy knee-length skirt and sleeves that came to the elbow. "Here, try this."

Kimber held it up and immediately I could see that Joan was right. With Kimber's reddish hair and fair skin, she'd look fantastic in pink.

"Try it on," I said.

"Well . . . I don't know if I should." Kimber turned toward a mirror with the dress in front of her, looking hesitant. "It's so different from what I usually wear."

"Nothing wrong with different," Joan said.

She studied the price tag. "It's expensive."

"You have babysitting money," I reminded her.

"Well . . ."

"Please," I said. "Keep me company."

"When you put it like that . . . okay." She grinned and hugged the dress to her chest.

Joan shot me an approving glance and I basked in it. Was this what it meant to be normal? Shopping with a friend—I'd never had one before—and with a mom who had enough money and confidence to try to bring out the best in a girl?

"I'll try it if you try on these shirts," Kimber said, gesturing toward the slinky ones.

"And try these, too." Joan held out an armload of black pants she'd been pulling off the rack.

It wasn't hard for them to convince me to head for the fitting room. When your main shopping experience has involved two-dollar, sour-smelling jeans from the Goodwill store, you can get high as a kite on the stiff feel and chemical scent of new clothes.

"Joan, you ought to try this on!" Kimber pointed to a fringed vest.

"I can't shop in the juniors' department," Joan said.

"Why not?"

"I'm president of the P.T.O. I have to look dignified." She fingered the vest.

Kimber snorted. "Mom says Mrs. Dixon wears miniskirts to all the parent meetings . . . and she's not half as skinny as you are."

"Yes, but at least Mrs. Dixon is young. I'm old. I have hot flashes. I should be shopping in Women's World!"

"No way," Kimber said. "That's where my grandma shops."

I took the vest off the rack and held it in front

of Joan. It had beads and wild colors and looked like pure fun. "You'd look great in it," I said, meaning it.

"Face it, Mrs. McGraw," Kimber said. "You're not the Women's World type. Just like I'm not the professor type."

"And I'm not the Goodwill type," I said.

"All right." She linked arms with Kimber and me and we marched into the fitting rooms.

I slid on a pair of tight jeans and smoothed down the slinky red shirt. Then I looked in the mirror.

This could not be me.

I looked like a girl in a magazine. My hair, which I'd always worn long, was now a sleek and shiny chin-length bob. That was because the stylist said I had a classic model's face, with "cheekbones to die for," and this haircut was supposed to emphasize it.

It did, I guess, but I felt weird without my long hair. My eyes seemed so big in my new, unfamiliar face.

And then there were these tight clothes, which both Kimber and Joan insisted were the style. I was used to baggy jeans and Mom's old shirts, clothes I could hide in. With these, there was nowhere to hide.

My chest, which had been growing for the past two years while the rest of me got skinnier and skinnier, jutted out embarrassingly. I definitely had to get some new bras if I was going to dress like this. The ones I'd shoplifted last year were already too small.

"Hey, are you dressed?" Kimber's voice came from the other side of the fitting room door.

"I guess so, but I don't feel dressed."

The door opened. "Good, because you've got to see—"

I met Kimber's eyes in the mirror. "What?"

"Joan, c'mere," she said. "Look at Rose."

"What?"

Joan crowded in and looked at me.

There was a funny little silence.

I couldn't read their faces and I was getting very uncomfortable about the way they were staring at me. "Okay," I said, "so the clothes don't work. I don't like them anyway. If I could just get a new pair of, you know, regular loose jeans and a couple of sweatshirts—"

"She's prettier than Mandy Patterson. And Mandy was homecoming queen."

"She's prettier than a model," said Joan. "Rose, you have a spectacular figure. I had no idea."

"You're so skinny! Do you diet all the time?"

"Um, no." For a genius, Kimber could be pretty dense.

Joan studied me, frowning. I knew she was worried I had some kind of eating disorder, but the fact was, I just wasn't used to having enough to eat. Now, when Joan put her big meals on the table, it was like my mouth didn't know how to swallow so much food.

I knew from looking at that weird Web site Fred had showed me that Dani had the opposite problem. She couldn't stop eating the food in her new foster home. Her cheeks and her pockets were always bulging with it. Poor kid: she was afraid she'd be hungry again.

I shook those thoughts away. "What happened to your dress?" I asked Kimber.

"Oh, I tried it. But I'm not sure."

"Put it back on!"

"Yes, do," Joan urged her. "I'm definitely getting the vest. Dale will like it, even if the P.T.O. doesn't."

But Kimber was still studying me. "Rose, you could get any boy you wanted," she said.

I looked at Joan. I thought a normal mother thing to say would be, "Don't focus on boys."

But Joan nodded proudly. "Newspaper or not," she said, "you'll be dating right away."

The way she said it gave me an idea. "So if I'm dating, everyone's going to think I'm normal, right? Like you and my social worker and the judge?"

Joan cocked her head to the side. "Doesn't every teenage girl want to date?"

That was my answer. For Joan, dating was the key sign of normalcy. So, like it or not, I had to date, and apparently these clothes and this hair-style were going to magically transform me into someone guys noticed.

The idea made me both excited and nervous.

Joan gave me more outfits to try and the two of them left the fitting room, jabbering away. And as I pulled on slacks and sweaters and skirts, the next step in my campaign clarified itself in my mind.

I had to date Brian.

If I dated him, I'd have a reason to hang out at his house and keep tabs on Dani, making sure she didn't forget where she really belonged. I'd get Joan to think I was normal, and she'd report that to Fred, who'd report it to the judge.

Not to mention the little shiver of excitement that passed through my body when I thought about Brian putting those muscular arms around me.

Of course, there was the small obstacle of his girlfriend. Mara wouldn't give Brian up easily.

And, though Joan and Kimber liked my new look, I still felt pretty abnormal. Why would Brian want to date me?

Maybe just acting interested in dating him would be enough for Joan to give me the thumbs-up as a normal girl.

There was a bang on the fitting room door and Kimber walked in, smiling but uncertain in the pink dress.

"You look great!" I told her as we stood side by side in front of the mirror. It was true. Finally Kimber looked like a regular teenager instead of like somebody's old aunt.

Kimber hugged herself. "Maybe, just maybe, I'll get a boyfriend," she said.

"You will. We'll make it happen."

Then she studied me. I had on the shortest of the skirts and a snug peach-colored sweater that gave my cheeks a healthy glow. "That's it!" she said. "That's what you've got to wear to the newspaper meeting next week. Man, I wish I could be there. You're going to be a big hit."

After the shopping trip, I felt weird, like some kind of alien to myself and my past. I kept getting surprised when I saw myself in the mirror. So I logged onto www.ALTLIVES.com to catch a comforting glimpse of Dani.

Only what I saw wasn't exactly comforting.

Five women, including The Witch, sat in a circle in the living room with Dani at the center. One smiled and nodded at Dani, even stood up and did a little jump in the air. The others, except The Witch, made notes on folders of paper.

Dani watched them, a wary expression on her face.

What were they doing to her?

Guilt flooded me. I'd been out having fun, enjoying my girls' shopping day, while Dani was being tormented by what looked like some kind of scientific test.

Another of the notewriters joined in, actually holding up one of Dani's legs and trying to get her to move that way. Dani was the clumsiest person in the world and she knew it. No way could she hop on one foot.

She was getting frustrated too. I saw that wild look come into her eyes and wanted to rush into the scene and wrap my arms around her—the best way to get her calm. But, of course, I couldn't.

I had to regain control of Dani's life.

But until I could, at least I'd try to hear what they were saying. I found the "audio" button on the screen and clicked on it.

Immediately the screen went black and my room was filled with sound.

"Her motor skills are way below normal, aren't they?" That was The Witch, sounding anxious.

"She has deficiencies, but that's typical with Down syndrome," said a cool, professional voice.

"Next," said another woman, "we'll do the self-care questionnaire. We'll mostly need for you to answer questions based on what you've observed in the last two weeks, ma'am."

"That's fine," The Witch said.

There was some shifting and shuffling, and I

heard Dani humming to herself. At least they'd stopped harassing her.

"Let's start with dressing herself," said the cool voice.

"Not at all," The Witch said. "She can't even put on her own socks."

"Can't or won't?"

"Well, you have a point. It's pretty clear she's never been taught even the basics. But she also has an attitude. It's like she doesn't want to learn."

I sat back in my chair, mad. That wasn't fair. Dani liked learning if you approached it right. And what was so hard about getting an eight-year-old dressed every day? Why couldn't The Witch just do it, if she thought she was so great with kids?

"Personal hygiene?" asked another woman.

"Nonexistent," said The Witch.

As they went on talking, I heard a banging sound, The Witch's quiet rebuke, and then shattering glass. Dani's loud wail followed.

"This behavior is typical, FYI," said The Witch, and there were more shuffling paper sounds as Dani's wail grew softer, then disappeared with the bang of a door.

"That is so not fair!" I yelled at the blank computer screen. Of course Dani was acting up. These people were ignoring her and talking trash about her at the same time. What did they expect?

"Everything okay in there?" It was Dale's voice, outside my door. Then the doorknob rattled.

"I'm fine! Don't come in!" No telling what would happen if Joan or Dale found out about the ALTLIVES game, but I knew they wouldn't like it. They were still on my case to make more friends. "I'm on the computer," I added, and in a moment I heard his footsteps retreat down the hall.

I turned back to the computer and switched to video so that I could see what was going on. Dani was back in the room now, subdued, and the women were holding out cards to her, their smiles fake. She clamped her mouth shut and turned her head.

I couldn't blame her, but at the same time I wanted her to pass whatever test they were giving. She wasn't dumb; she understood more than you'd think.

The worker shook her head and started loading cards back into a briefcase.

Dani reached past the worker's hands and grabbed a storybook. I watched The Witch spin around, ready to scold her. But Dani's face lit up and she started pointing to the pictures and talking.

I tried to see what the book was about; I couldn't, so I switched back to audio.

"The princess, she stuck in tower," Dani said. "See? That lady say she the mommy, but she a witch. She climb up on princess's hair. Ouch!"

Tears came to my eyes, hearing Dani recount the Rapunzel story we'd read together so many times. I always said, "Ouch" at just that point.

"Look, there the prince. See? *P* for prince. Just like princess, *p*."

"What's that letter, Dani?" asked one of the women. Her voice was excited now.

"That *a*. See? And that one *d,* for Dani. Me!"

There was the sound of pages turning and murmurs of approval. "Can you find the horse on this page, Dani?"

"That not a horse. That a unicorn. See? Big horn."

A couple of the women laughed, and there was a lot of talking and paper-shuffling. "Clearly, someone's been working with her," someone said.

"A lot more potential than I thought."

"This is something to build on."

"Such a shame she wasn't in early intervention."

"I'm going to recommend an extra focus on reading at school."

"But she still qualifies for help with her other delays, doesn't she?" Of course, that was The Witch, sounding all anxious.

"Right, there are a lot of concerns. But we

want to build on strengths, not just remedy weaknesses. This is very encouraging."

I logged off the game with a big smile and a, "Go, Dani!" Thank heavens she'd happened to find that storybook. Dani and I had spent hours every day reading fairy tales; they'd been our salvation when we were trapped in our dark apartment. Through them, we'd escaped into a fantasy world. I was glad these professionals appreciated all that Dani knew.

But as I thought about what I'd seen and heard, doubt crept into my mind.

I was proud of Dani for showing that she could identify pictures, tell stories, and read some letters. But there had been such a huge contrast between the way the testers had acted during the first part of the hour and the last part. I realized how negative their earlier attitude had been.

Maybe I should have tried harder to get Dani to learn how to do things for herself. Maybe I should have spent more time trying to get her to move and run.

I'd done the best I could. But had it been good enough?

Chapter Five

When Joan dropped me off in front of Brian's house the next Wednesday night, I heard a group of boys laughing and felt terminally shy. Why had I ever agreed to do a school activity?

Brian stood in front of his house, gesturing us to a side door. "This way to my bachelor pad," he said. He was joking, but he sounded nervous. Odd.

When he saw me he looked puzzled for a moment, and then his jaw dropped. "It's you," he said. "You cut your hair."

My hand flew up to it and I nodded.

We stood staring at each other.

From the side of the house, I heard a girl's voice. "Okay, I think everyone's here except that . . ."

And then Mara came around to where we

were standing. "Who's *that?*" she asked, approaching Brian and putting her arm around him.

"It's Rose. She got her hair cut." Brian shook his head fast like he was waking up out of a dream. "Let's go down and get started."

"Where's Dani?" I asked him as we headed down the side stairs.

"She's getting ready for bed," he said, his voice low.

"Dani? At seven thirty?" That was weird. Back home, she wouldn't even consider going to bed until ten or so. But then we always had plenty of time for a nap during the day if we wanted it. It wasn't like we were going anywhere.

"We won't see the kids," Brian said, still quietly, "at least not if I can help it."

I opened my mouth to protest, but as we walked into the basement study, the other teens' curious stares made me retreat into silence. No one said, "New girl!" but I felt like that was what they were thinking.

A few of them had seen me before in classes or walking around the halls of school. But they hadn't paid a bit of attention to me in my old sweatshirts and baggy clothes.

Obviously, my makeover had changed everything. Joan would be thrilled, but part of me longed for my old clothes and hair to hide behind.

Brian took advantage of the temporary hush. "Okay, everybody. Koonan couldn't come, so we're on our own. Koonan's our advisor," he said to me, then turned back to the whole group. "Tonight I want to assign beats for the semester and talk about our meeting schedule."

"Who's your friend?" a kid asked, gesturing toward me.

"This is Rose Graham," Brian said. "She's new at school, and she wants to work with us."

"Cool!" said the boy, with a little bit of a leer.

"Yeah," said another.

I just wished they'd stop staring at me.

Apparently Brian did too, because he gave them a dirty look. "Listen up. The basic beats are boys' sports, girls' sports, clubs, school news, and town events. Then we've got room for a column, since Laurie had to quit. Any calls?"

"Boys' sports," said one of the boys who'd spoken up before.

"I want girls' sports," said the leering guy.

"Sorry, Matt. I want a female to cover that."

"That's a problem," said a tall, thin guy. "There's only two girls here."

"Mara," Brian said, "would you want to cover girls' sports?"

She shook her head. "I'm no jock," she said. "I want to do a social column."

"Well, you play tennis," Brian said. "It's a good beat."

"Brian," she said in a warning tone, like she was his boss or his wife.

51

need a girl who will."

"How about Rose?" she asked.

I lifted my hands. "I don't know anything about sports," I said. "Sorry."

"Nothing?" he asked, and then nodded as if the memory of my background had just clicked into place. "Oh, right."

Mara gave him a dirty look and I knew why. He hadn't prodded me about not doing sports, the way he did to her.

He glanced away from her. "Okay, we'll come back to girls' sports. What about clubs?" And he went on distributing the beats.

I was trying to figure out how to get upstairs to check on Dani. It was hard when Brian had set things up to be completely separate. He had music playing, so you couldn't hear a thing from upstairs. There were a couple of bags of potato chips and a cooler of soft drinks, so I couldn't claim hunger or thirst to draw me up to his kitchen.

Hearing my name brought me back to the present. "Rose and I still don't have beats," Mara said. "Does that mean I get my column?"

"Social columns are boring," said the thin guy. I'd figured out his name was Tim.

"Rose, what do you like to write?" Brian asked. It was clear he didn't know what to do with me.

"She's the only one who gets what old Tomkins is talking about in English," said one of the guys. "Too bad we don't have a Shakespeare beat."

My face warmed as everyone looked at me. "Um, maybe there's important stuff going on at school outside the regular beats?" I asked. "Maybe I could just be, like, an extra."

"You've never even been to school before," Mara said, "so how could you know what's important?"

"You've never been to school?" asked Tim.

"Not for a long time," I said, feeling my face get hot.

"She's like this alien," Mara said, raising her fingers behind her head like antennas. A couple of the other kids laughed.

I wanted to crawl under the beat-up couch and hide.

Brian snapped his fingers. "An alien," he said, looking at Leonard, a smart kid with glasses who was taking notes on a laptop.

Leonard cocked his head. "Interesting."

"What could we do with it?" Brian grinned at him. It was clear they were used to brainstorming together.

As I watched them, my embarrassment gave way to an idea. Wouldn't Leonard be a great boyfriend for Kimber?

"How about a column, 'The Alien View'?" Leonard suggested. "What Linden High looks like from the outside. What it would be like to come here from Mars."

Brian bit his lip and glanced at Mara. It was clear that he liked the idea.

"But there's only room for one column," Mara said, "and I want to do the social scene."

Leonard made a sound like a buzzer blaring. "Forget it, Mara. No one wants to read about who wore a blue dress or who was seen with whom at Tommy's Pizza."

Oh, I liked him. He'd be perfect for Kimber.

Mara obviously didn't share my good feelings. "Well, nobody wants to read about some alien like *her.*"

"Mara's right," I said. "Nobody would be interested in me." I felt like the little mouse princess in Dani's favorite fairy tale, too scared to play the game and win the prize.

But I wasn't the mouse princess. I was stronger than that. "I have another idea," I said. "I think a column like 'The Alien View' could be interesting if it covered all the outsiders. You know, like the kids who aren't popular. Or kids who are different. Like, say, Kimber."

Brian nodded. "It could work."

"It'd be great," Leonard said.

"You only think that because it would be about your geeky friends," Mara said.

"I'd read it." A heavyset guy in a beer T-shirt gave me an approving look. "Finally, something different from every other high school paper in the country."

"I'm smelling a National Youth Press award," Leonard said, smiling at me.

A warm glow spread through my chest. They liked my idea!

"Well, I think it's ridiculous. No one wants to read about a bunch of weirdos." Mara stood up. "I wonder if I'm even needed here." There were tears in her eyes.

"Hey," Brian said.

"I'm leaving." She grabbed her coat and headed for the stairs.

Brian rolled his eyes at the other kids. "I'll be right back."

"Aw, lover's quarrel!" someone called, and there were kissing sounds all around. But it was friendly. I could tell everyone liked Brian.

Against my will, I liked him too. Enough that I wished he didn't have a creep of a girlfriend like Mara.

The heavyset guy burped loudly. "Gotta hit the head," he said, and lumbered up the stairs.

The head . . . an old military movie we'd watched on cable came back to me. The head was the toilet.

Aha. My route to Dani.

As soon as the heavy guy came back down, I started for the stairs. Unfortunately, Brian and Mara were coming back in, so all eyes turned to us.

"Where are you going?" Brian asked.

"Is there a charge to use your bathroom or something?" I snapped, and to my surprise everyone laughed.

I went on up, ignored the bathroom I saw, and followed the voices to the upstairs rooms of the house, tiptoeing and hugging the wall.

I could hear Brian's mom in the upstairs bath-room, and some splashing. Was she bathing Dani?

I crept into a bedroom where a crib and a funny bed with a crank and screens around it each held a kid. But not Dani. "Who're you?" asked a boy.

I smiled at him as I backed out. "A friend," I whispered, and closed the door gently.

In the next bedroom I saw two twin beds—and Dani sat on one. She was looking at a color-ful board book, and when the door opened she glanced up.

And then she looked back down.

My heart twisted. She didn't recognize me

with my new haircut! Why, oh why, had I let Joan talk me into a makeover?

I opened my mouth to speak to her, but just then I heard the bathroom door open. I stepped into the room and quickly closed the door.

Immediately, it opened behind me. Hands on both of my shoulders pulled me out while Dani continued studying her book, unaware.

"Who are you?" hissed Brian's mother, a.k.a. The Witch, with a slightly hysterical edge in her voice. Then, after she studied me, she said, "Oh. You."

It was like she'd have preferred a prowler.

I put my hand back on the doorknob to Dani's room. "I'm checking on my sister."

"You can't just walk into someone's house! And you're not to see Dani for another week. She needs to get settled here." The Witch paused. "I'm half tempted to call the police."

"But I'm here for a meeting with Brian!" I protested. "I'm on the newspaper! I didn't break in."

"Mommy!" came a voice from the bathroom. The flat, babyish voice of a kid like Dani.

"You get downstairs to that meeting and leave Dani alone," she said. "No more sneaking around. Understand?"

"Can I still see her in a week?" I asked. It hurt so much to be this close to my sister but not able to see her, examine her, talk to her. I needed a hope. I wasn't faking the tears in my eyes.

Her lips tightened and she studied me. After a thirty-second staring match, her eyes softened. "If you can encourage her to settle into our home, then yes," she said. "She's doing well here, Rose. You need to get behind that."

I nodded and forced myself to turn and walk down the stairs.

The meeting downstairs had broken up. Brian had his arm around Mara as he talked to a couple of the guys. The rest of the kids milled around, joking and eating potato chips or talking on their cell phones.

I'd told Joan to come get me at nine. That was ten minutes away, and I sat down in a corner, feeling awkward and lonely.

It was strange: I'd spent so much time alone, but I'd rarely felt lonely. Now, in a room full of laughing, normal teenagers, I felt like crying with sadness.

Sure, I'd gotten a makeover. And I was participating in a school activity.

But inside I felt just as abnormal as ever.

I couldn't help but watch Brian and I saw a look of dismay cross his face. He let go of Mara and headed over to the stairs. Some of the other kids looked that way, too.

And then I heard it: the voice I loved more than any other.

"Where my Rose?"

Immediately I shoved through the crowd of kids to where Dani stood about four steps up, surveying the room. "I heard my Rose upstairs," she said. "Where my Rose?"

She was adorable in footed pajamas, her face flushed, hair still damp from her bath. "Hi, honey," I said, opening my arms to her. "It's me."

Puzzled, she studied me for a few seconds, and then recognition brought a huge smile to her face. "Rose!" she cried, and launched herself into my arms. I staggered under her weight, and the guy named Tim caught and steadied me.

"Who's this?" he asked.

"Nobody," Brian said. "Never mind."

"She's not nobody, she's my sister," I said, hugging her tight.

"Oh my gosh, she's drooling!" Mara said.

"Shut up," I told her, wiping Dani's mouth with the back of my hand.

"That not nice," Dani scolded me, and several of the kids laughed.

I tottered backward and sank down onto the couch with her in my lap. "How are you doing? Are you okay?" I asked her.

She nodded. "I okay. But where you go, Rose? Why you run away?"

My heart lurched and I stroked her face, trying to keep back my tears. "I didn't run away, honey. I want to see you. But your foster mom says I have to wait a little while." I paused while she studied my face and played with my hair. "Are you having fun here, Dani? Are they nice to you?"

She nodded. "They have lots of food here. And lots of toys."

My sigh whooshed out of me. "That's good."

"Who these people?" Dani asked, and for the first time I realized that the entire crowd was circled around us, listening.

"They're, um, Brian's friends," I said.

"I like Brian," Dani said. "But Brian not like me."

I glanced up at Brian, who looked mortified. "Time to go upstairs, Dani," he said, trying to lift her off my lap.

"I want Rose," she said, clinging to me.

"Give us a minute," I said to Brian.

"She's not allowed down here. She knows that!"

Dani started to cry. "I need my Rose!"

"Thanks a lot," I said to Brian.

"How'd she find out you were here, anyway?" he asked, his hostile whisper barely audible over the sound of Dani's wails.

"None of your business." I pulled Dani back onto the couch and rocked her back and forth. It was the same way I'd always calmed her down, but it didn't work as well when there was a mob of people around us.

"Well, get her out of here. Now!"

"Jeez, Brian," Tim said. "Have a heart. She's your sister?" he asked me.

I nodded.

"And she's living here?" He looked puzzled.

"Foster kids," Mara explained with a raised eyebrow.

"Hey, Rose," someone yelled from upstairs. "Your mom's here."

I perched Dani upright on my knees, facing me, and wiped her tears with my thumbs. I looked hard into her eyes. "I'll come back and see you again real soon, okay?"

"I go with you?" she asked in a plaintive voice that wrenched my heart.

"No. You have to stay here for now."

"I no want to stay here." She flopped forward and clung to me.

There was a commotion on the stairs and then The Witch was there, hands on hips. "What is she doing down here? You're not supposed to have contact. You know this!" She reached down and somehow pulled my sobbing sister from my arms. With a practiced move she held Dani facing away, one arm across her chest and the other under her. That way Dani's kicking feet couldn't hurt her.

"This," she said, nodding down at Dani and then looking at me, "is your fault. She's been perfectly happy for days."

Brian's glare was an echo of his mother's. The other kids were turning away, looking embarrassed.

I'd never felt more like an unwanted outsider.

Chapter Six

"So how's your plan to start dating?" Kimber asked as we pushed two wheelchair-bound girls out into Linden High's recreation area early the next week.

I'd started going with her to volunteer in special ed, partly because it got me out of study period and partly because it helped my loneliness from missing Dani. There were some Down syndrome kids there, and somewhere inside me I thought that if I helped and comforted them, someone at Dani's new school would help and comfort her.

But today we'd been assigned a couple of snooty girls. They didn't want us to play with them; they wanted to talk by themselves. So we pushed them into a sunny corner and left them, and then stood shivering on the other side of the rec area.

"I don't know how to start dating," I told Kimber. "If someone asked me out, I'd probably have a stroke."

"What if it were Brian?" Kimber knew about my secret crush.

"Mara's stuck to him like Velcro. I never see him alone. Not that he'd ask me out anyway."

"Hmmm." For once Kimber didn't know what to say.

"How about you and Leonard?" I asked. "Did you talk to him at lunch?"

"In the line," she said, "but then he went off with these chess club guys. There was no way I could horn in on their table."

I'd told her I thought she should go after Leonard, and after I described how he'd brainstormed with Brian and nixed Mara's social column, she'd agreed he might be a good first-boyfriend target for her. The problem was getting to know him without obviously chasing him.

And for me to advise Kimber about dating was fairly ridiculous: the blind leading the blind, or in this case, the homeschooled leading the homeschooled.

Still, I had to try. "Are you in classes together?"

"Duh. We're both in Honors everything."

I clapped my hands. "You two are so perfect for each other. Can't you, like, drop something on the way out of class? Or ask him for help with homework?"

"That kind of stuff only works in books," she said. She shrugged, her face and eyes doubtful. "Maybe I'm just not meant to have a boyfriend."

I went behind her and straightened her slumped shoulders. "Take a deep breath and repeat after me: 'I'm funny and pretty and I will get a boyfriend.'"

She giggled, but she did it. And then she said, "How though, Rose?" with a plaintive, wanting tone that reminded me of Dani.

"I don't know how yet. But we'll figure it out. I promise."

We watched a teacher play catch with two Down syndrome girls. One of them caught the ball easily, while the other kept missing, getting frustrated, and crying. The teacher was great; she kept the girls talking and playing, and when the clumsy girl finally caught the ball, all three of them were thrilled.

"That one who's having trouble, Cindra, is from a real deprived home," Kimber explained. "Her parents never worked much with her or had her in a program or anything. But since she's been here, she's been catching up."

My stomach did a flip-flop. Kimber could have been talking about Dani.

She looked at me and then clapped her hand over her mouth. "Oh my gosh, Rose. I keep forgetting you're from a deprived home too."

"Yeah, but I'm catching up," I said sarcastically.

"I'm sorry." She paused and then, being Kimber, went on talking. "You know, I'm curious about how you managed with Dani and all that. Joan told me your mom was, like, out of it."

I shrugged. "We got by," I said.

"Yeah, but how? How'd you know how to take care of yourself and a sister with Down syndrome too?"

I leaned back against the cement wall. "It's not like Mara says. We weren't raised by wolves. When we were younger, Mom was better. I went to elementary school, and Gram taught me to read and cook and stuff. We were fine."

"But Social Services took you away," she said.

"Right, because after Gram died, which was two years ago, we didn't have much money. Mom got disability checks and checks from the state for Dani, but she couldn't go out to cash them, so—"

"What do you mean, she couldn't go out?"

"She was—" I swallowed. "She was scared to leave the house and she slept all the time."

"Depression? Agoraphobia?"

I shrugged. I didn't know what agoraphobia was, but I didn't want to seem stupid. "I guess."

"So you just did it all yourself?"

"Yeah, but not always all that well. Like, I could take a check with a note from her and get it cashed, but after her driver's license expired and the tellers we knew got laid off at the bank, it was harder. And then we'd run out of money, and I'd have to . . ." I shot a glance at her, then looked away. "I had to steal. That's how I screwed up, actually. I got caught stealing food."

"Wow." Kimber shook her head, her eyes round. "That must have been awful."

I thought back. Had it been awful? "At least Dani and I were together," I said.

"But that's the other thing. I can't imagine having the full responsibility for a kid with Down syndrome. I mean, they're sweet. But it's so hard to teach them anything."

I swallowed a scared, sour taste and lifted my face to feel the wind. "I didn't teach Dani that much. Even basic things, taking care of herself . . ." I shrugged. "I was always there to help her brush her teeth and get dressed and all of that. We tried to learn a little bit of reading, but that's about it." I waited for Kimber's reaction. She worked with special ed kids; she'd know if I'd been a bad big sister.

But she shrugged. "You're just a teenager, Rose. People go through years of training to learn how to teach special ed."

I nodded and tried to immerse myself in the sounds of the recreation yard: shouting and bouncing balls and teachers' encouraging voices. But I couldn't eliminate my nagging new fear that I hadn't done enough for Dani.

So was my goal of getting my family back together the right thing to do?

"Tell me more about the newspaper column you're doing," Kimber said.

And as I explained it to her, surrounded by the special ed kids, I flashed on the topic for my first column: "The Alien View: Special Ed."

Two hours later, I sat in the newspaper office writing my column.

I did fine with starting a new file and roughing out the first couple of paragraphs, but then my computer ate a great sentence. I made a disgusted sound.

The other kid in the office came over. "What's wrong?" he asked. "You're Rose, right?"

I recognized him from the meeting at Brian's house. He was the one who'd told Brian to have a heart. "Yeah," I said.

"I'm Tim," he reminded me. "How's it going?"

I explained my computer problem and he showed me the "undo" function to get back the text I'd lost.

But he didn't go back to his project after he'd helped me. Instead he leaned against a neighboring desk and asked, "So, what're you writing?"

"It's a column about special ed kids," I said, turning back to the screen. I really wanted to get my ideas down while they were fresh.

"Really? That's cool." He bent to look over my shoulder. "My cousin's in special ed here."

"Oh yeah?" I tried to keep typing, but having

him there made me self-conscious, so I turned around to look at him.

He was tall and dark-haired, with freckles sprinkled across his nose. A little lankier than Brian, but cute.

"Uh-huh." He shifted from foot to foot. "Hey, you want to go to a party this weekend?"

My eyes widened. "You're not . . . asking me out, are you?" I couldn't keep the shock out of my voice.

His face reddened. "I guess I am," he said. "Is that a mistake?"

"No, it's just . . . I'm not used to it." I was too surprised to be embarrassed or shy. "I'm really not that big on parties."

"Sure." He turned away, jamming his hands into his pockets.

He was hurt. Hurt, because I'd seemed to turn him down! "Wait, Tim," I said.

He didn't turn around.

"I could give it a try," I said. "I just . . . you've probably heard the rumors about how I grew up, right? So I'm not used to a lot of people. I can't guarantee how long I can take a big crowded party."

By the end of my speech he'd turned back. "That's okay, Rose," he said. "I think it's kind of cool you've never really, you know, done any-thing before." His face turned red again. "I mean, like parties and stuff."

Why did I feel the urge to rescue him? I was supposed to be the shy one. "I think it'll be fun," I said. Which wasn't true, but it would help me achieve my goal of seeming normal. "Thanks for asking me."

"Sure!" he said.

Suddenly I got a brainstorm. "Hey, will Leonard be there?"

Tim shrugged. "He'll be invited, but he's just as likely to stay home and read his encyclopedia or do science experiments."

"What if he knew a girl who liked him was coming?"

"He'd be there," Tim said, "if only because of the novelty. Girls hate Leonard."

"You get Leonard there and I'll guarantee him an interested girl," I said.

"Okay," Tim said doubtfully. "But it'll be a real partying party, if you know what I mean. It'll be great, but . . ."

I didn't know what he meant, but before I could ask him about it, Brian walked in. "What'll be great?"

Tim gave Brian a "none of your business" look.

As for me, I was still mad at Brian for the way he'd treated me and Dani at his house. "What's great is this column I'm writing," I said. "You'll love it."

"What's it about?" he asked.

As soon as I told him the special-ed premise, he shook his head. "That won't fly," he said. "No one wants to hear about those kids." He walked over to his desk—unmistakable because of the big "Brian Johnson, Editor" sign on it—sat down, and started flipping through a stack of mail.

Hallway noise had died down as kids left school. The only sound in the office was from Tim's clicking keys; he'd gone back to his work.

But Brian's attitude hacked me off. I stalked over to his desk, planted my hands wide, and leaned toward him. "You're the only one who doesn't want to hear about special ed kids," I said. "You're selfish and arrogant and you think no one's interested in anyone who's not all perfect, like you!"

He glanced up, then back down at the mail in his hand, continuing to rifle through it. "That's not true," he said. "I'm just tired of them getting all the attention."

"They don't get any attention!" I grabbed the mail out of his hand to force his attention on me. "They're off in a separate wing of the building and you could be here for a year without knowing they're around."

He was looking at me now, those chocolate eyes full of a strong emotion I couldn't identify.

"We're not running it," he said. "Write something else."

"You can't do that," I said, slamming my handful of his mail down onto his desk. "You can't just give a flat-out refusal to a story because of your personal prejudice."

"I'm the editor, Rose."

"And you're pulling rank?" I put all the disgust I could muster into my tone.

"Uh-huh."

We were staring at each other. I knew I was leaning too close to him, talking too loudly, breathing too hard, but I was so mad! This obnoxious, mean person was living with my sister. I wasn't even allowed to see her, and he was living with her.

And he was preventing me from writing stories about people like her. It wasn't fair.

To top it off, he smelled good! It was an earthy, piney scent, and I didn't know if it was soap or aftershave. Did he shave? I looked at his cheeks and upper lip and saw a faint stubble.

His eyes broke away from mine and skimmed down my body. It was just the quickest of once-overs; I wasn't even sure that's what it had been, because he looked back at my face right away and then turned to look at the wall.

But something about it made me remember that I was wearing my new, tighter clothes and that Kimber and Joan had raved about how pretty I was.

I straightened up, crossed my arms over my chest, and took two steps back.

"Geez, Brian," Tim said in a mild voice. "If it were me, I'd let Rose do anything she wanted."

"Why's that?" Brian snapped.

Tim gave me a little smile and a wink. "Oh, lots of reasons."

"Give me one."

Tim paused, and I was suddenly afraid he was going to tell Brian we were going to a party together. For some reason, I didn't want Brian to know.

"Well," Tim said slowly, "remember the gay rights rally last year?"

"Yeah, so what?"

"Well, remember Koonan didn't want us to cover it?"

"Where are you going with this, Tim?" Brian asked.

"When they threatened a lawsuit, he caved," Tim said.

"Right, and?"

Tim shrugged. "Seems to me special ed kids have rights too," he said.

"Oh, and you think they're going to threaten us with a lawsuit?" Brian asked sarcastically. "Like they're really together enough to do that?"

"Looks like they have a pretty together advocate," Tim said, giving me a warm smile.

"Why are you standing up for her?" Brian asked.

"Why are you attacking her?"

"I don't know," Brian said, and turned back to his work.

Suddenly I was tired of being the "her" they were talking about as if I wasn't even there. "I'm writing the story," I said. "And since the deadline is tomorrow, and you've saved space for my column, and this is the only thing I'm turning in, I guess you'll just have to run it."

Brian ignored me.

But Tim gave me a thumbs-up as he gathered his stuff to leave the office. "See you Saturday," he said. "I'll pick you up at seven-thirty, okay?"

I blushed and glanced at Brian, who was staring at us, looking puzzled.

"Sure," I said. And then I lifted my chin, sat back down at my computer, and proceeded to type my story, giving Brian the silent treatment. Let him see how it felt to be ignored.

Chapter Seven

At seven-fifteen on Saturday night, I was a mess. I couldn't believe my first-ever date was going to start in just minutes.

What did people do on a date? What did they talk about? Would Tim want to kiss me?

Would I let him?

Or was this all a big joke? Had he just been teasing the new girl? Would he not show up at all?

I could have talked to Joan about my worries. She would have loved it. But she was so hyper that she would have just made me more nervous, so I hadn't even told her about the date. I had been hoping she and dear old Dale would be out with some of their many, many friends by the time Tim arrived, but I could hear them talking above the TV sounds downstairs.

That just added to my anxiety.

The only thing that made me feel good was

Kimber. She was thrilled to be going. We'd rigged a conversation in her parents' hearing about how I was so scared to go to my first high school party because of my pitiful family background. Kimber had comforted me and said she'd like to go to support me, but wasn't sure if her parents would allow it.

After she did some heavy talking with them about her religious duty to help others, they'd agreed she could go.

But I was still terrified.

To calm down, I logged onto ALTLIVES.com and asked to see what Dani was doing.

A shaky video image showed Dani in the kitchen with The Witch and one other little kid, a boy. The two kids were up on footstools, one on either side of The Witch. I watched while she opened a canister and said something to the boy. He nodded, scooped out a cup of flour, and dumped it neatly into a big bowl on the counter.

Dani started crying and grabbing for the cup. She wanted a turn too, I could tell. But it would be disaster to give her one. Her hands were nowhere near as steady as the other boy's.

To my amazement, The Witch handed the cup to Dani. She scooped flour out, too eagerly, and knocked over the canister.

I just knew The Witch would retaliate. But to my surprise, she shrugged her shoulders, smiled at Dani, and helped her scoop a cupful of flour from the pile on the counter. She guided Dani's hand to the bowl and helped her scoop it in. All three of them clapped madly, and Dani looked thrilled. Then the kids took turns stirring the mixture in the bowl.

I couldn't stand to watch anymore. It was great that Dani was getting to help around the kitchen. She'd actually done better than I thought she could. But that raised the uncomfortable idea that I'd been holding her back. Maybe my expectations had been too low. We'd sure never had enough food to let her mess around and ruin some of it while learning to help cook.

"I want to see Brian," I typed. I'd never asked the computer this before and I wasn't sure what would happen.

You are authorized to view family members only, the computer told me.

Rats! Without really thinking, I typed in, "That's not fair."

You may receive a transcript of what others in the household are doing, the computer responded.

Now that was weird. It was like the computer didn't want to be called unfair and had made a compromise with me.

Was that possible?

Curious, I typed in, "Okay, I'll take a transcript on Brian."

Immediately, lines started appearing on the screen.

A young man sits in the darkened living room. Occasionally he gets up to look out the window. He glances often at his watch.

So Brian was waiting for something. What? Probably for Mara to arrive. And didn't it just figure that he was all by himself, instead of helping out with the cooking or the kids. The jerk.

It occurred to me that I was being a jerk, too, by invading Brian's privacy. But I couldn't seem to stop myself.

More lines appeared.

Headlights flash in the front window and the young man rushes to look out. Then he returns to his chair, turns on a reading light, opens a file folder, and begins to study the papers inside.
The front door opens and a man enters.
"Hi, Dad," the young man says.

I wished I could switch to video. This was the first I'd heard about the father of the household, and I was curious.

"How's life at the paper?" the young man asks.

"Fine, fine." The older man hangs up his coat in the front closet. "Where's your mother?"

"In the kitchen. But, Dad—"

The man is halfway across the room. He pauses. "What?"

"When you have a minute, could you give me some advice about something at the paper?"

The older man looks puzzled. "What do you have to do with the paper?"

The young man is silent for a moment, then says, "The school paper, Dad."

"Oh, that's right. I'd almost forgotten you took it over. How's it going?" The older man continues walking toward the doorway into the rest of the house.

"It's going well, but . . ." The young man breaks off.

"Good, good," says the older man over his shoulder as he leaves the room.

"Dad!"

"What?"

"I'd appreciate a little bit of your time!"

"Later, all right?" The older man looks back into the living room. "You know, I expect you to have some patience." He leaves the room.

"Right. I have to be patient because I'm the normal one." The young man sighs, looks at *his watch, and walks upstairs. "I'm going out now, Mom and Dad," he says to the empty upstairs hallway. "To a party where the parents aren't home. There'll probably be drinking and drugs, but don't worry. I can hold my liquor." He goes into his bedroom and slams the door.*

Well, that was depressing. What good was it to have a father if he completely ignored you?

And what party was Brian talking about? Surely not the same one Tim was taking me to?

I asked the game to switch back to Dani and video. But that wasn't much more cheerful. Dani was sobbing on a chair in the corner, and from reading her lips, I could tell she was begging for a cookie.

The Witch was pretending to ignore her, although she looked upset as she put dinner on the table. When Dani got up out of the chair and ran toward a tray of cookies, The Witch took her by the shoulders and guided her back into the chair. It happened again, and the Witch put her back again.

Dani started wailing. I could tell that the volume was extremely high.

The Witch bit her lip and spoke to the man of the house who'd just come in. "Harder on me than on her," was what it looked like she was saying.

Yeah, right! Couldn't my sister have one cookie she'd helped to bake?

I had to get Dani out of there.

I glanced at my clock radio. Seven twenty-nine. Was Tim the type who'd be on time? I wiped sweaty palms on my jeans and hoped I'd chosen the right outfit.

Since Tim wasn't here yet—was he standing me up?—I decided to take a quick look at Mom. I typed the command into the computer and waited for the usual dark screen to come up. Mom didn't turn on a whole lot of lights.

But today she was up out of bed and talking on the phone. I could count on one hand the number of times she'd taken a phone call in the past year. Of course, she didn't have me to take care of things for her, so maybe she'd been forced to become more active.

Which might be good. Sometimes this ALT-LIVES spy game made me wonder if I'd just screwed everything up by trying to take care of my family myself.

I studied Mom. She looked about the same as when we'd left, except that she had on slacks and a shirt that could conceivably be worn out of the house. In the months before we'd left, she had rarely gotten out of her nightgown.

She hung up the phone and went to a cupboard, and I watched nervously to see if she had enough food to eat. I saw a couple of cans of soup and a box of crackers. Stuff I hadn't bought, so she must have either gone out or had someone bring her food. I'd have to check with old Fred and see if he'd followed up.

At least she wasn't starving. I watched her open the soup can and felt my usual mixed feelings about her. She was my mom, and I missed her. But she hadn't really acted like my mom for a long time. When I had one of those "I need my mommy" moments, the person I missed was Gram, not Mom.

Out in front of the house, a car door slammed.

I shut down the computer and ran downstairs. "I'm going out," I said breathlessly to Joan and Dale as the doorbell rang.

"Whoa, Little Missy. Going out where?" Dale asked.

"To a party. With Tim. He's a boy who works on the paper with me."

"You have a date?" Joan clapped her hands together. "Rose, that's wonderful!"

"See you later," I said, turning toward the door.

"Now wait a minute." Dale folded up his paper and stood. "We have to meet your young man."

"That's right," Joan said as she walked behind me, talking all the while. "Why didn't you tell me you had a date? I could have helped you get ready. I always helped Michelle get ready for her dates. This is so exciting!"

"Yeah, too exciting." I felt like I was going to get sick.

Joan stopped me with a touch to my shoulder, turned me around, and studied me, her head cocked to one side. "Good choice of outfit. That shirt Kimber picked out suits you," she said, giving me a warm, Joan-style smile. "You look just right."

Her words settled my pounding heart.

"Deep breaths," she coached as we turned toward the door. "You're going to have so much fun."

Dale invited Tim in, and he came and sat down in the living room. After a few minutes of getting-to-know-you small talk, he told them about the party we were attending: where it was, who was likely to be there, how long it would last.

"We haven't even talked about a curfew," Joan said, frowning at Dale. "What do you think?"

"Eleven o'clock?" he said.

"I'm only fifteen," I said. "Ten would be fine." I couldn't imagine staying at a party or talking with Tim, whom I barely knew, for four hours.

The three of them laughed like I'd said something funny. "Ten or eleven, then," Joan said to Tim.

"And no drinking," Dale added. He put a hand on my shoulder. "If you need a ride home, you call us."

I felt so weird as I walked out the door with Tim. All mixed up with my anxiety about my first date was this warm fuzzy feeling of family. Joan and Dale were watching out for me, and they knew about teenagers. There was no way my mom would have known what to say to a teenage boy.

When Tim and I arrived at the house where the party was, I knew right away that the parents couldn't be home. There was a cooler full of beer in the kitchen and kids were smoking on the back porch. It was a lot more crowded than I'd expected, and I knew almost no one. I looked around for Kimber, but didn't see her. I hoped her parents hadn't changed their minds.

"Want some punch?" Tim asked, pointing to a cut-glass punch bowl filled with pink liquid.

"Sure," I said, relieved. So he wasn't going to offer me a beer. He'd listened to Joan and Dale.

Tim handed me a paper cup of punch and then turned to greet a couple of people he knew.

I took a drink and choked.

Someone handed me a napkin and patted my back, and when I recovered, I realized it was Brian. "I wouldn't drink too much of that if I were you," he said.

"What's in it?" I sputtered out.

84

"Grain alcohol, I think."

I'd never heard of it. I watched Tim down his cup and pour himself another.

"You having fun?" Brian asked me.

"Um, we just got here." I didn't know how to feel about Brian. On the one hand, I was still mad about how he'd acted toward my column on special ed kids. On the other hand, having seen him try and fail to get his dad's attention on ALTLIVES, I felt sorry for him.

Complicating all of that was the odd way my heart pounded just from being near him. It was so crowded at the party that Brian stood with his chest brushing my shoulder. His arm was sort of around my back, too. It felt wonderful. I could have leaned into him and stayed there for hours, and I didn't even know why.

Tim turned and saw us standing together, and elbowed his way through the crowd. "Hey," he said to Brian in a less than friendly voice.

Brian took a half step away from me. " 'Sup," he said.

Then the two of them did some weird grunting and nodding and backslapping thing that seemed to make them feel more comfortable with each other.

A couple other people who wrote for the paper came over, including Leonard and then a girl from my math class. Though I didn't talk much, I felt friendly with these people, and they seemed to accept me as one of them. Maybe it was because I was standing here with Tim and Brian, but I seemed to be passing for normal.

Not only that, but I was even having fun.

Until Mara came over.

Apparently she'd been delayed by a big, fancy party her parents were having, and she had to brag about the caviar and champagne they were serving and all the people arriving in evening clothes. "It was totally boring," she said, sounding fascinated with her own story.

She kept touching Brian—fixing his hair, brushing something off his shirt, nuzzling up against his side. It was like she was plastering him with a thousand little Post-It notes that said, "Mine."

It didn't seem to bother him one bit.

The group we were talking with started drifting off. When Tim suggested that we go outside, I was glad to. I'd had enough of watching Mara and Brian together.

As we started to go outside, though, Kimber came in the front door. Her cheeks were flushed from the cold, her eyes wide and excited. And when she shrugged out of her coat and revealed her pink dress, I almost clapped. She looked normal . . . and really, really pretty.

"Kimber!" I called, and looked around for Leonard.

He was deep in conversation with an overweight boy who had a bad case of acne. More evidence that Leonard was a nice guy, but I had to get him to look out for himself. "Get Leonard over here," I whispered to Tim.

"Why?" he whispered back.

"Because Kimber's here."

"Kimber?" Tim gave me a disbelieving look. "Is that who you're setting Leonard up with?"

"Uh-huh."

He started to say something, caught a glimpse of Kimber, looked at me, looked at her again, and looked at me with raised eyebrows. "I'll get him."

Kimber reached me a few seconds later. "Oh my gosh, I thought I'd never get here. My parents wanted to drive me, but I knew that would be a disaster. They'd want to meet the parents and everything. I told them I was walking and picking you up." She looked around. "This is so cool. My first party outside of church!"

"Tim's getting Leonard," I said.

"What?" she squealed, grabbing my arm. "Not yet! I'm not ready! I don't know what to say to him. My hair's a mess!"

"It looks good that way," I told her, straightening one strand that was falling down in her eyes. "The wild look. I think it's, well, sexy."

"Oh my gosh. Really?"

I couldn't help laughing. "I think so, but how would I know?"

"How's it going with Tim?" She studied me. "You look great. Are you having fun?"

"Kind of," I said, "but not because of Tim. I mean, he's nice and all. A really nice guy. But . . . I don't know." I glanced around the room.

Kimber read my mind. "He's not Brian."

"Right. And Brian's here. With Mara." I nodded in their direction.

"So make him jealous," Kimber advised. "Give Tim a chance. Oh my gosh, here they come. I am so nervous. Do you think Leonard knows I like him?"

"Um, probably."

She clung to my arm for support, and I found I didn't mind. I'd never realized how nice it could be to have a friend, especially now as I faced all the scary stuff of high school.

"Hi, girls," Leonard said. He sounded cool and calm, but I noticed that there were beads of sweat on his forehead.

"Hey," I said.

Kimber didn't speak. That was so unusual that all three of us looked at her.

She had a smile frozen on her face and a slightly crazed expression in her eyes. Her hand clamped my arm tighter, practically cutting off my circulation.

If I didn't do something, she was going to ruin her chances with Leonard by acting all weird. "Um, you have to excuse Kimber," I said. "This is her first high school party and she's a little out of her depth." I looked at Leonard. "She just needs some help getting oriented."

"Orientation I can do," he said, squaring his thin shoulders. "Now, on your right, you see a pink punch bowl. It looks completely innocuous, but notice the victims passed out on the floor . . ."

"Victims?" Kimber asked in a high, shrill voice. "Oh, you're joking." She let out a giggle.

Leonard looked sideways at her. His quirked eyebrows said he was willing to reserve judgment.

"On your left," he continued, "you'll notice Brian and Mara feeding each other cheese curls. Their close proximity suggests that they have not yet had their fight-of-the-night. We have major entertainment ahead, ladies and gentlemen."

"I can't wait," Kimber said, rolling her eyes at me. Her voice was back in its normal range, and her vise grip on my arm loosened.

Tim was chuckling. "Leonard's got things under control," he said close to my ear. "Let's go outside."

I didn't exactly want to. I wanted to stay and support Kimber. But she had to sink or swim on her own, so I peeled her hand off my arm and followed Tim outside.

Even though it was pretty cold, with a light layer of snow crunching under our feet, there were some other kids outside. The smokers were on the side of the house, laughing and talking. Others were mostly in couples, scattered around the tree-lined yard.

Making out.

My heart started beating really fast. Was that what Tim had in mind too?

I didn't know how I felt about that. I liked him, but I hardly knew him.

I certainly didn't feel the quivery, excited feeling that came to me whenever I was around Brian.

He led me over to where a trellis arched against the garage. Reaching over, he plucked a flower and handed it to me.

"Here's a rose," he said, "for a rose."

It was so sweet and so romantic! It was just like something you'd read in a fairy tale.

I smiled at him. "Thanks."

He put his hands on my shoulders and backed me against the wall. "You are really pretty," he said.

Then he kissed me.

I was so shocked at how fast it happened that I didn't have time to get that nervous. I just stood there, surprised that his kiss was kind of wet. I guess it was because his mouth was open and mine wasn't.

So this was my first kiss. I had to admit, I was

underwhelmed. Was there something wrong with me, that this wasn't making me feel anything?

He pushed his tongue between my closed lips, just a little, and I automatically turned my face away. "Sorry, Tim. I don't want to."

He was breathing hard. "Why not, Rose? I really, really like you."

"I'm sorry. It just . . . I don't . . ."

"What?" His eyes were hurt.

I felt terrible. Who would have guessed that dating could be so hard, that it might involve me causing pain to someone else? "I'm sorry," I repeated.

"If it's just because you've never dated before, we can go really slow. We don't even have to kiss. We can just hang out here and—"

"I don't think so, Tim." It was weird. I had no experience, and I liked Tim a lot, but I knew without a doubt that I'd never have that boyfriend-girlfriend feeling with him. I stepped sideways, wanting to get back into the house.

"Hey, c'mon, let's just stay here and—"

"No, Tim," I said as gently as I could. "I want to go inside."

For a minute I thought he wasn't going to move; then, suddenly, he was jerking backward, a surprised look on his face. Then I heard the hard *thwack* of a fist connecting with his chin.

Then he was on the ground.

"Didn't you hear the lady?" Brian growled. "She said no."

My hero! I walked out from under the trellis where I'd felt trapped. "Thanks," I said, "but you didn't need to hit him." I started to kneel down by Tim, but he waved me away.

"Don't you know any better than to come out here with a drunk boy?" Brian asked as I stood back up.

"He's not drunk," I said. "He had a couple of cups of punch, that's all." I could hear kids yelling, "Hey, there's a fight!" over the sound of Tim's moaning.

"You should be more careful. And don't even think about riding home with him."

Brian was sounding less and less like my knight in shining armor and more like some kind of big brother. Which irritated me, but I wondered if he meant to offer me a ride home himself. That would be, well, very nice.

He pulled a cell phone out of his jacket pocket. "Now, what's your phone number? I'm calling your parents."

Kids were approaching from all over as Tim got to his feet. But I was too disappointed to care who heard us arguing. "Why? So you can tell them someone was kissing me?" I took a step closer to him. "Listen, I might be naïve about high school customs, but I know a kiss on a date is no big deal."

"Yeah, Johnson. What the hell did you hit me for?" Tim sounded slurry and dazed.

"Brian!" came a familiar shrill voice. "Are you okay? Someone said you were fighting!" Mara rushed over and started examining Brian, who was of course completely unhurt.

"I'm fine," he said, twisting away from her.

"Why are you and Tim fighting?"

"He's got some bug up his rear end about Rose," Tim grumbled. "Jeez, can't a guy get a private minute with his date around here?"

Mara turned and saw me. Light dawned in her hostile, rapidly narrowing eyes. "You brought this on."

"Excuse me?"

"I know what you're trying to do."

"I'm trying to go out in a normal way, without anyone pressuring me or hitting my date or yelling at me."

To my surprise, a bunch of the kids surrounding us laughed.

But as the group broke up and Tim stumbled inside for ice, as Brian called Joan to come and get me and then disappeared back into the house with Mara, as Kimber waved from across the yard and then disappeared into the shadows with Leonard, I kept wondering. Why had Brian hit Tim?

Was he just playing big brother? Or could it be that he felt the same kind of shivery pleasure around me that I felt around him? Enough that he wanted to hit a boy who was kissing me?

And why did that thought put such a thrill in my heart?

Chapter Eight

If I'd thought my campaign to date Brian would speed up, I was wrong. After he hit Tim at the party, Mara shortened his leash. I only saw him at newspaper meetings and in the office, and even there, Mara stuck to his side like an evil fairy.

He edited my columns and ran them without comment. After special ed, I covered foreign students, those taking honors classes, and the gay-straight alliance. Even though that last one generated some controversy, he didn't discuss it with me.

My visits with Dani didn't bring us together, either. The Witch insisted on supervised, one-hour visits in the playroom of the local Social Services office, claiming that was what the judge and my social worker had advised.

Of course, I wanted to visit Dani at her new home. Not so I could see Brian, though that would have been nice, but so I could check out Dani's life and be a part of it.

Finally, late in March, I scored an invite to Dani's house. Dinner with the whole family wasn't my first choice; I would have rather taken Dani off by herself to play.

But this was all I, or rather Joan and Dale, had been able to arrange. So there we sat: me, The Witch, Brian's dad, Brian, four retarded—oops, developmentally delayed—kids of preschool and school age, and Dani.

At first The Witch wasn't even going to let me sit next to Dani. Something about consistent routines: Dani usually sat between two of the other kids, and a change wouldn't be good for her.

Like The Witch hadn't caused the biggest change of all, keeping me away from Dani!

But Brian and his dad made her see reason, so there I sat, helping Dani eat spaghetti. The meat sauce smelled rich and the bread I'd grabbed a bite of was hot and buttery. Judging from the enthusiastic grunts and food-smeared faces, the kids surrounding us liked the meal too.

Brian looked miserable, and I didn't know why. He seemed embarrassed about the younger kids' table manners, but surely he wasn't worried about what I would think. I'd grown up with Dani eating like an animal.

Maybe it was the dad thing. He kept trying to engage his father in conversation, but between the noise level and his dad's apparent desire to get progress reports on each of the younger kids, he didn't have much success.

"Here, let me cut that," I said to Dani as she slurped a mouthful of spaghetti.

"No, I tirl it," she said, pulling away from me. "Watch." She started twisting her fork in her dish.

"It'll work better if—"

"Dani's been learning to twirl her spaghetti," The Witch explained.

"What do you mean?"

"Not of Italian ancestry, eh, Rose?" asked Brian's dad. He demonstrated on his own plate, twirling a forkful of spaghetti against a big spoon and then lifting it to his mouth.

I looked around and saw that Brian and his mom were eating the same way. Even the littler kids were making attempts to do it. I was the only one with a plate of neatly cut-up spaghetti in front of me.

Had I been eating spaghetti wrong all along? Why hadn't Mom ever told me?

"Dani can't do that," I said to cover up my embarrassment. I reached over and cut her some bites, over her protests.

"She can't if you never let her try." The Witch sounded almost sad.

"Fine. Let her spill her food all over herself. I'm not doing her baths and laundry anymore." That

97

reality choked me up, so I backed off and watched Dani.

What I saw amazed me. She wiped her own mouth, used a fork most of the time, and drank milk out of a regular cup without spilling it. She also talked to the other kids, to Brian's parents, and to Brian, whom she seemed to idolize.

The truth was, Dani seemed to be doing well here. So well she was in danger of forgetting who she was and where she came from.

I spoke to her in a low voice. "I bet Mom would love this dinner," I said.

She looked at The Witch with a puzzled expression, and then at me.

"I mean our real mom, not her." I nodded toward The Witch. "Remember how spaghetti could sometimes make her come out of her bedroom to have dinner with us?"

Dani nodded. "Mommy like sketti!" Then she frowned. "Where Mommy go?"

I glanced around. Brian sat slumped and sulky, and his dad was eating and helping one of the more disabled kids eat.

The Witch was watching me and Dani.

I gave her a snotty look. What right did she have to spy on me and my sister? It was bad enough that we were only allowed supervised visits, since everyone was afraid I'd throw Dani in the back of some truck and take off. But couldn't we at least have a private conversation?

If not, then she'd have to take the consequences. Including the fact that I was going to talk about my real mom.

"Mom's back home," I told Dani. "Back in our apartment. Remember? With the blue couch and the windows looking out into the street and the MacKenzies yelling upstairs?"

Dani's eyes filled with tears and she put down her fork. "I sad, Rose. I miss our mommy."

I rubbed her shoulders with one hand. "Me too, honey. Me too. But we'll go back there someday to live. Someday soon, I hope."

"Rose," said The Witch, "would you please help me bring in the salad?"

"I can help, Mom," Brian said.

"I asked Rose." Her voice was tight.

Brian shot me an apologetic look as I stood and followed The Witch into the kitchen.

She spun and pointed a long bony finger at me. "I won't have you upsetting Dani. There is no point in that."

"I'm not trying to get her upset."

"She was crying! She's barely cried in the past week."

"That's not true." I cut myself off. I knew through ALTLIVES that Dani cried whenever she had to go to the time-out chair, which was pretty often. But I couldn't admit I'd been spying. She'd probably have me thrown in jail.

The Witch poured salad dressing onto a big

bowl of greens and started tossing it with two big wooden forks. "Look, I know she needs to stay connected with her birth family," she said. "But let her settle in here, Rose. She's doing very well."

That phrase "birth family" put a chill in my heart. Mom and I were Dani's family, period. "She's only here temporarily," I said. "Pretty soon, we'll be back home with our real mom."

She handed me a stack of little plates. "Don't get your hopes up," she said, and headed back to the dining room ahead of me.

Don't get your hopes up? What was that supposed to mean?

We *were* going home, and soon. The Witch just didn't want it to happen. She had a control thing going on and plus she was probably getting attached to Dani. Who wouldn't, as sweet and cute as she was?

At the table, The Witch started firing questions at Brian's dad about his work at the newspaper, all the while dishing out plates of salad and passing them around. Clearly she wanted to make it impossible for Dani and me to have a private conversation.

The dad started talking about a troublesome reporter whose ego was getting in the way of his work. "He wants to sit in his cube and write personal essays, but that's not the way we operate. I need him on news."

"I have the same problem at school," Brian said. "Someone who wants to write a column and won't cover her beat."

I got interested despite myself. I knew Brian was talking about Mara.

"This guy actually turned down an assignment today. Turned it down!" Brian's dad shook his head.

"Why don't you fire him?" The Witch asked.

"Can't. Politics."

"My advisor won't let me fire anyone either," Brian said. "He's so happy when anyone signs up to work on the paper that we're stuck with them, no matter how bad they are."

I crunched on a carrot and watched to see if Brian's dad would pay attention to what Brian said.

He didn't.

"F-f-f-fire!" exclaimed one of the kids, a boy who looked to be about six. "I like f-f-f-fire."

"Good talking, Saul!" The dad reached over and ruffled the boy's hair.

What about your other son's talking? I wanted to ask. *He's actually saying something!* "Brian does a great job as editor," I said to Brian's dad.

"Really? Oh, careful, Saul. Don't forget to chew!" He patted the younger boy's back.

"Did you know he quit baseball so he could edit the paper?" I asked.

"Who did?" Brian's dad tipped his head back to study me through his glasses.

"Your son," I said, nodding at Brian. "Gave up the thing that makes high school kids popular so he could edit the paper, which doesn't."

"Doesn't what, dear?"

"Make kids popular."

He nodded encouragingly at me. "That's a good observation," he said with a complete lack of understanding of what I'd said.

The Witch was sharper. "Brian wasn't raised to care about popularity," she said. But it didn't sound like praise for Brian; it sounded like praise for herself, for how she'd raised him.

I looked at Brian, but he wasn't looking at me. He stared at his salad, poking it around in his bowl.

I felt bad for him. He was basically a good kid. I mean, he'd driven me crazy at the party the other night, punching my date and bossing me around, but it all came out of trying to help me. He wasn't smoking and drinking.

His parents, though, barely noticed him. They were too caught up in the younger kids and their problems.

Finally dinner was over and all the kids tried to take their own dishes to the kitchen. That meant a lot of silverware, dirty napkins, and leftover bits of rolls and spaghetti landed on the floor.

When I tried to take the dishes away from the clumsiest of the kids, The Witch jumped on me. "Let him carry it, Rose. We're teaching them to be self-sufficient, which means cleaning up after themselves."

"Doesn't that make a lot more work for you?" I was genuinely puzzled by her attitude, especially since she was so uptight about so many things. How could she tolerate a messy floor?

"It's more important that they learn."

"My job, put forks in washer," Dani said. She climbed up on a step stool by the counter and started grabbing silverware. The next minute she was holding it under the faucet, spraying water and bits of food all over herself and the counter.

"No, Dani!" I grabbed the forks away from her.

The Witch held out her hand for the forks. When I gave them to her, she handed them right back to Dani. "Hold them down lower, like this," she said. "That way the water won't spray."

"I like 'pray," Dani said.

"Well, I don't," The Witch said. "And if you do it again, you'll go to the time-out chair."

I waited for Dani to kick up a fuss. She hated being threatened. But to my amazement, she carefully rinsed the forks, stepped down from the stool, and put them into the dishwasher.

"Now I wipe off chairs," she told me proudly.

She grabbed a sponge and headed back toward the dining room.

I was about to follow her when the little boy Saul came in carrying two half-full glasses of milk. Both slanted at precarious angles while the milk sloshed around.

"Whoa, Saul, let me help," I said, and took the glasses from him.

The Witch spun from the sink. "All right, fine. Kids, you all have the night off. Rose is going to help me with the dishes."

"Yay!" cried one of the kids who'd been collecting paper napkins to throw in the trash. She dropped them on the floor and ran off toward the sounds of a Disney video.

I picked up the napkins and dropped them in the trash. I didn't say anything, figuring I was about to get some kind of tongue-whipping from her. And I was right.

"Let's just have it out, Rose," she said, banging pots and pans in the sink. "It's clear you're trying to undermine me at every turn. What I don't understand is why."

I started loading glassware into the dishwasher. "I'm actually trying to help you and the kids," I said. "I don't know why you have to take it the wrong way." Even as I said it, I knew it wasn't exactly true. I would've liked to undermine The Witch if I could think of a way to do it.

"We have a philosophy of parenting in this

house," she said. "We teach our children to be as self-sufficient as possible. The goal is independent living at some point, and they'll never get there if we infantilize them."

"If you what?"

"Treat them like babies. Do everything for them." She leveled a glare at me. "Take the dishes out of their hands and clean up after them. Cut up their spaghetti."

"Oh." I could see that she had a point, though I wasn't going to admit it to her face.

"If you want to visit Dani," she continued, "you need to support our goals for her. So what's your problem with all this?"

Her bossy tone infuriated me. "My problem," I said, probably too loudly, "is that you're not her mother. And you're not my mother. And I really don't appreciate your acting like you're holding all the cards."

She laughed in a bitter way. "Foster parents don't hold all the cards. And neither do you, for all your attitude."

Attitude? She thought I had attitude? "Who does, then?"

"Believe it or not," she said, "your mother."

Chapter Nine

"My *mother?*"

I heard myself bark out a laugh. The image of Mom having any kind of control of anything was just too weird.

"That's right. It's up to her to meet whatever goals the judge set for her as conditions to get her children back."

"Why didn't my caseworker tell me?" It wasn't like I saw Fred every day, but we'd spoken on the phone several times and he'd visited once. Never had he mentioned any kind of conditions on my mom. He'd just told me that a community program was helping her with grocery shopping.

The Witch handed me a dish towel and a big kettle. "You haven't heard about it because it's about your mom, not you."

"But Mom can't meet goals by herself," I said.

"If she's got some kind of test to pass, I have to help her."

She bit her lower lip and shook her head. "That's just it, Rose," she said almost gently. "You're only fifteen. You're not the head of the family. You've been taking care of things you shouldn't have to worry about. So the courts took that responsibility away from you and put it back where it belongs, on your mom."

"But she can't do it!" I banged the kettle down on the counter.

"You didn't think Dani could eat by herself or help with the dishes, either," she said. "Maybe you've been underestimating your mom."

"So it's my fault my family's the way it is?"

She closed her eyes for a short space of time, shaking her head. "That's not what I meant."

I grabbed another cooking pot and started drying it. "How is she supposed to show she's met her goals? And when?" I was thinking of what I'd seen on ALTLIVES. Mom sure didn't seem to be making big changes.

"There's a court date set to review her progress," she said.

"When?"

"Well, your first hearing was in January. So it's sometime in April."

"But it's March now!" I couldn't believe this. "You're telling me," I said, just to make sure, "that no matter what I do, even if I prove to my social worker that I'm all normal and everything, it's not going to make any difference? It's all about Mom?"

She put her hand on my shoulder. "Calm down. Your caseworker will give his report, and that will have some impact."

I was breathing hard and tears pushed against the backs of my eyes. It was like time had slowed down to a crawl. I could hear the kitchen clock ticking and the rowdy sounds of kids in the TV room. I smelled the lemony dish soap as I twisted the thick, damp dish towel in my hands.

I couldn't look at Brian's mom, the bearer of all this bad news. Instead, I stared at the black-and-white linoleum floor until its patterns seemed to shift and swirl beneath my feet.

"Surely you can see," she went on, speaking carefully, "that if both you and Dani are doing well in your placements, but your mother hasn't made any changes, it wouldn't make sense for you to go back to the exact same life you were living before? A life even your mother knew was bad for you?"

"What's that supposed to mean?"

She reached into the soapy dishwater, opened the drain, and watched the suds drain out, fishing a stray fork from among them. "You know, your mom agreed to relinquish you into care," she said. "This didn't happen against her wishes."

"That's not true." I collapsed back against the counter, staring at her.

"Yes, it is."

"She wanted us out?"

"She called Social Services herself after the police brought you home from your latest episode of shoplifting."

"I have to go," I said, putting the dish towel carefully on the damp counter, avoiding her eyes. "Please tell Dani I'll see her soon. Thanks for dinner." And I turned and ran out the back door into the cold darkness.

Running and crying occupied all my attention for at least ten minutes. But eventually my sobs and gasps and tears slowed down.

At which point I noticed footsteps.

Heavy footsteps. Heavy breathing. A few yards behind me.

All the scary stories Gram used to tell me about the world outside our apartment came back. There were a million bad things that could happen to little girls, she'd said, and most of them involved bad men who followed you in the darkness and did unspeakable things.

Linden Falls wasn't the same as my run-down, crime-ridden city neighborhood; there were no gangs of teenage boys hanging around the street corners, no raucous drunken parties spilling out of apartment doors.

But in a way, this cold silence was worse. There was no one here to help if whoever or whatever it was came closer.

I started running again.

"Dammit, Rose, wait up!"

It was the only voice that could have soothed me. I spun around.

Sure enough, there came Brian. Relief washed over me.

"Why'd you . . . run off . . . like that?" he complained as he caught his breath. "I'm always having to rescue you. When are you going to learn to take care of yourself?"

My relief turned to irritation. I didn't want him to see my swollen, red-eyed face, so I wheeled away from him and started walking toward home. "Nobody asked you to sneak up on me like a serial killer!"

"Actually, Mom asked me to walk you home. And to bring you your coat. Here."

I shrugged into it. "Oh, and you always do what Mommy says?"

"You shouldn't be out here by yourself," he said. "Especially since you're upset." He reached over and brushed the back of his hand over my wet cheek.

I sucked in my breath. Wow! To cover up how

good his tender touch made me feel—after all, he did have a girlfriend—I made my voice harsh. "You aren't my big brother. You don't have to take care of me!"

"You seem to need it," he said. He didn't sound irritated anymore, though. He actually sounded like he liked protecting me, but I couldn't believe that was true. Probably just wishful thinking on my part.

"I'm fine," I said.

"You're not fine. What happened?"

I took a deep breath in and let it out slowly. "Your mom just told me some things I didn't know."

"Like?"

"Like, my mom gave us up voluntarily. She didn't want us!"

"Come on, let's walk," he said, pulling me around until we faced the same direction. "Maybe she just knew she needed help."

"So she shoves us out of her life?" I shook my head. "No, Brian. That's just wrong. It was bad enough that she couldn't take decent care of us, but this!"

"You said it yourself: she couldn't take care of you." He grabbed my hand and pulled me into forward motion. "So what else is bothering you?"

"Isn't that enough?"

"Yeah, but—"

"I also found out I have no control over my life." I told him about the court and how my mom had to meet some kind of conditions in order to get us back. "It's probably something like showing she can shop for food, and get us to school, and do her own banking. Stuff she hasn't been able to do for years. There's no way!" I had to stop talking or I would've started bawling again.

"What's wrong with her?" As we walked, Brian picked up a rock and tossed it in the air, over and over.

"Good question. Kimber thinks she's agoraphobic, or depressed, or both." I'd looked up both conditions on the Internet, so when Brian looked puzzled, I explained, "Agoraphobia is this anxiety thing where you're afraid to go out of the house. And depression . . . well, you know. Bad mood, tired but can't sleep, eating problems. When it's clinical depression, it goes on and on and affects your relationships and daily life."

"She never saw a doctor?"

I shook my head as guilt churned in my stomach. Why hadn't I tried to get her to see a doctor? "Mom's just different," I explained, as much to myself as to Brian. "That's what Gram always said. It's not something you can fix." As I heard

113

my own words, despair swirled around me like a dark, heavy cloud.

We'd always known Mom couldn't get better. That was just a fact of life. She only ever got worse.

So what were the chances she could meet some court-ordered conditions that would let us get back together as a family?

And what were the chances she'd even want to?

"You might be wrong about her. Maybe she just hasn't gotten the right help before."

I shook my head. "Thanks, but I doubt it."

We walked a few minutes in silence. I snuggled into my coat and let the frosty air cool my hot cheeks. A car drove by slowly, then pulled into a driveway in front of us.

Brian glanced at the car, ducked his head, and walked faster. A moment later, he took my hand. "So why don't you just stay in Linden Falls and get happy about it?"

I stared at him. "What do you mean?"

"If there's nothing you can do about your situation, why don't you just stop fighting everyone and settle in?"

I jerked my hand away and turned to face him, hands on my hips. "You can't possibly understand."

"Try me."

"No way." I spun away and started walking fast. But as he caught up to me, I couldn't keep quiet. "You have a family. You've always lived with them. You can't possibly imagine what it's like to have your family ripped apart."

"Living with your own family isn't always so great," he said.

"What do you—" I stopped as the dinner scene I'd just witnessed replayed itself in my mind. It was true: Brian didn't have it easy. "I guess I see what you mean. Hey, how come your parents take in kids like Dani, anyway?"

He sighed. "After me, they tried forever to have another kid. Mom finally got pregnant, but Micah was born with Fragile X. It's kind of like Down syndrome, a genetic thing."

I nodded. There was a kid who had it in the special ed class.

"Anyway, once they figured out how to cope with Micah, they decided it was their mission to take in more kids like him. Mom's good with them."

I wasn't sure about that, but I wasn't going to badmouth his mother. "Doesn't leave much time and attention for you," I said.

He shrugged. "You want to stop at the playground?" he asked, gesturing toward a small park tucked between the houses and the shopping district in town.

"Why?" I asked.

"Haven't you ever gone back to the places you used to play as a kid? Swung on the swings and slid down the slides?"

"Um, I didn't play on playgrounds that much as a kid."

"Why not?"

I shrugged. "Just not that into it." Which wasn't exactly true. I felt, or remembered, a funny kind of longing as the swings and slides came into view.

"You've gotta like swings!"

He grabbed my hand and pulled me toward the jungle gym that loomed in the darkness ahead of us. "Now, we have to be quiet," he said. "The park is supposed to close at dark and the cops started patrolling after some kids were caught drinking here."

"I don't really feel like playing kids' games," I said. But I let him drag me along.

The truth was, I liked having him hold my hand. And I liked the piney-smelling soap or aftershave he used. I actually leaned a little closer so I could get a better whiff of him.

At the swing, he sat me down, pulled the seat back, and let it go. I lurched as my body tried to remember the childhood moves.

"Let yourself go!" he said, laughing.

I held on, and he pushed me, then he jumped

onto the neighboring swing and pumped until he was flying high.

After a couple of minutes I was soaring back and forth, clutching the metal chains in my hands.

Being here made my body remember a time, way back, when Mom was well and Gram was healthy and they took me to the park to play. I got a sudden flash of my mom's face, laughing, planting a kiss on my cheek each time I swung forward. How old had I been? Three? Four?

Tears stung my eyes, maybe from the cold air, maybe from the memories.

Each time I swung forward, I caught a glimpse of a sky full of stars. And it was like they were talking to me. They said things like:

We were here when you were a kid and we're here now.

We'll be here when you're old and all this is in the past.

There are things that are bigger and more important than your problems.

"Hey," Brian called after a little while. "Are you zoning, or what?"

I was, and I didn't want to come out of it. But his words brought me back to the here and now, which surprisingly wasn't that bad of a place to be either.

"Come on, try the slide next," he said.

The ladder to it seemed to go on forever.

"What's the matter?" Brian teased behind me—close behind me—as I slowed down. "You scared?"

"No!"

He moved closer until he was on the step below me, his body wrapping around mine, warm and protective. "Don't worry. You won't fall. I've got you."

I stopped completely. My heart was beating hard, but not from fear.

No, I felt weird with Brian so close behind me that his breath warmed my neck.

He touched my hair, then brushed it back. His face was right next to my cheek, and I could hear his breathing. "Sure you're not scared?" he asked.

I climbed fast, out of the circle of his arms and up to the top of the slide. I heard him climbing behind me. I looked down the shiny expanse, which seemed slick and steep and dangerous. Then I thought about how it had felt to have him close to me, and that felt even more dangerous.

I slid down.

And landed hard on my butt.

"Ow!" I got up, just in time to keep Brian from landing right on top of me, and rubbed my sore rear end. "That hurts!"

"Want me to rub it for you?" he asked with an exaggerated leer.

"No!" I backed away from him, laughing.

"Are you having fun?"

I thought about it then nodded.

"Good," he said. "Playgrounds are great for forgetting your troubles." He gestured toward the slide. "Go on, try it again. I'll stay down here and make sure you don't fall."

I ran to the slide and started climbing. I felt like a kid, eager to get to the top, eager to feel the exhilaration of a fast ride down.

It made me think about Dani. She would have loved this playground. Maybe The Witch brought her here; in fact, probably so. The Witch knew what kids liked.

I didn't like her or her house, but I had to admit that it looked like a fun place to grow up. They had a whole room full of toys: a play kitchen, a plastic washer and dryer, kid-sized tables and chairs, a ton of dolls, and crafts. There was a little basketball hoop in the driveway, and bikes and balls and sleds in the garage.

No wonder Dani was having a hard time remembering home. Our apartment was like a cave compared to Brian's house.

"Come on down," Brian called from the bottom of the slide, and I realized I'd been sitting at the top for a couple of minutes.

I breathed in cold air and listened to the wind stirring tree branches.

"I'll catch you," he said.

I let go and slid, fast and free, laughing, cool air bringing a flush to my cheeks.

At the bottom, Brian caught me in his arms.

And he didn't let go.

Chapter Ten

My laughter died out as I caught the look on Brian's face. Was it admiration? Lust?

His hands still clutched my upper arms and even through my coat I felt their strength. We were standing close enough that I could see the streetlight reflected in his dark eyes.

Oh, Lord. He was going to kiss me.

I flashed back to when Tim had kissed me, all sudden and open-mouthed.

Was this going to be another bad kissing experience?

But Brian took his time, looking into my eyes. I guess he saw that kissing was okay with me, that I wanted to do it too, especially when I sucked in a breath and lifted my face to his.

He pressed his lips to mine, gently, moving a little bit, cradling my head in his hands like I was some precious, fragile thing.

It was heaven.

After a minute he lifted his head and smiled at me. "There's something about being with you," he said. He paused, thought, and spoke again. "Looking through your eyes is like seeing everything new."

Emotions swirled through my body. I could only breathe in short, shallow bursts. Being this close to him, feeling his warm touch, hearing his husky voice, smelling the warm, soapy scent of him . . . it was almost overwhelming.

Almost but not quite. I reached up and touched his lips with one finger.

"You're irresistible," he said, and kissed me some more.

My coat came open and his hands eased around me inside it, hot against my waist and back. His mouth tasted minty, delicious.

By the time we pulled apart, we were both breathing hard.

"Irresistible," he said again.

"You too," I panted. "Should we resist?"

Our eyes met and held. There were so many problems with our getting together. So many things we disagreed about. There was Mara.

On the other hand, kissing and touching and being close felt so good.

Even just holding each other like we were doing now felt so good.

And then, with one shrill shout, everything went bad.

"Brian!"

It was Mara's voice. Seconds later we could see her through the darkness—face contorted, marching stiffly and rapidly, eyes narrowed.

We jumped apart.

She stood with her hands on her hips, staring at us. "So it's true," she said. "I couldn't believe it when Sara called and told me she'd seen you together, holding hands."

"I guess that *was* Sara's mom's car I saw," Brian said weakly.

Mara wouldn't allow the interruption. "She said you were headed this way." She gave Brian a scornful glare. "I figured you'd come here, since this is your favorite make-out place."

I took a couple of steps backward. "You've brought other girls here to make out?"

Brian stepped back, lifting his hands like he was trying to fend off both of us. "Now wait a minute," he said.

Mara looked at me with a sneer. "What'd you think, that you were the only girl he'd ever kissed here?"

I didn't want to admit it, but I had thought exactly that. It had seemed so special, with him showing me the playground stuff. Was that all a big fake?

He gave me a pleading look, like he felt bad, and then turned to Mara. "Look, I can explain all of this. But I need to get Rose home. My mom will kill me if I don't."

He made it sound like a big obligation he didn't want.

"Oh, so you were just walking her home because your mom said to? Did she tell you to kiss her too?"

I'd heard enough. It was pretty clear that Brian was choosing to placate Mara, that hers were the feelings he wanted to spare. Maybe he'd gotten carried away in the atmosphere of the playground—who knew it was so romantic?—but now that his head was clearing, he had his loyalty to Mara.

Well, fine. I wasn't going to stick around and watch the teary reconciliation. "I can make it home myself," I said.

Secretly, inside, I was hoping he'd protest.

He didn't.

I turned and ran like a little kid, tears rising in my eyes again.

I wandered the streets for over an hour before going home, made excuses when Joan asked questions, and played sick the next morning. When I finally stumbled out of bed after noon and went downstairs, Joan was waiting for me.

"You have to talk to me," she said. "I know

something happened, and I'm not going to keep covering for you if I don't know what it is."

"You've been covering for me?" I asked.

"Yes, young lady, I have." She clunked a plate down in front of me: a turkey sandwich on whole wheat, an apple already cut up, and potato chips. "I covered with Dale when you weren't home on time last night, and I called the school for you this morning."

"Thanks," I said, taking a bite of the sandwich.

She poured me a glass of cola from a big bottle. "You're welcome. Now, what happened at Brian's house that has you so upset? Is your sister okay?"

I was pretty upset, and what harm would it do to talk? So I told her what The Witch had said about Mom giving us up voluntarily. "She wouldn't make that up, would she?"

Joan shook her head. "No, that's my understanding too. Your mom didn't feel she could adequately care for you, so—"

"So she put us out on the street!" I squeezed my eyes shut against the pain of it.

"More like got you off the street," Joan said. "Rose, you were living in a dirty apartment. You had no money. And your mom couldn't see any way out of that, so she got some help. I respect her for that."

"I hate her for it!"

"No, you don't." Joan patted my arm and

then walked over to the coffeepot to get herself more coffee.

As long as I was spilling my guts, I figured I might as well tell her all of it: what The Witch had said about Social Services, and the court hearing, and Mom. "Is that true, do you know?" I asked her. I didn't have a lot of faith in Joan's knowing the system, since she was new to foster parenting. But she and Dale had to take some classes to get approved.

She nodded. "Yes, I do know there's a hearing next month. I can try to find out more, but Brian's mom is right. You aren't the one who has to prove something. Your mom is." She touched my arm hesitantly. She was such a hugger, but I'd made it pretty clear I didn't like her brand of affection. "Is it so bad here, Rose? Do you really want to leave?"

"It's not that," I said, trying to put my feelings into words in a tactful way. "You and Dale are great, but Mom and Dani are my family. Just like Michelle loves Penn State, but her home base is here."

Understanding lit her eyes and she nodded. "I'll do whatever I can to help you, Rose. You're a little bit of a puzzle to me, but I do care."

"Thanks." To the surprise of us both, I reached over and squeezed her hand.

She got tears in her eyes, but she blinked them away fast. "All right. Finish your lunch, and then we're going to make cookies. And you're going to tell me the rest of what's bothering you."

So we hung out for the rest of the afternoon in the kitchen. Through the red-checked curtains, you could see gray skies and flurries of snow. Joan put the radio on to some oldies station and hummed along to songs Mom used to like too: Beatles and Rolling Stones and Grateful Dead.

We measured flour and sugar and butter and mixed them all together in Joan's fancy electric mixer. Then she showed me how to roll out the dough and cut it into pretty shapes with her massive set of cookie cutters.

Joan told stories about her own mom and grandmother, how they'd taught her to cook in this very kitchen when she was a little girl. And that led me to talk about my gram.

"She's the only reason I have a clue about anything," I explained as I cut a row of star-shaped cookies. "She took me to Sunday school so I'd meet other kids, and she ran a day care in our apartment for a while." I thought back. "She even started a Girl Scout troop in our building, hoping Dani and I would make some friends."

"Did it work?" Joan asked.

I shrugged. "Not too well. Dani acted so crazy and Mom hated having other kids in our place by then."

Joan patted my back on her way to put a tray of cookies in the oven. "It sounds like your gram did a lot for you girls," she said. "I bet you miss her."

"Uh-huh." But for once, thinking about Gram made me happy instead of sad.

I thought of Dani, making cookies over at The Witch's house. And here I was making cookies with Joan. Was this a regular thing that families did together, or only in Linden Falls? Even when Gram was alive, I didn't remember doing any baking. We got our cookies from the discount shelf at the store.

A warm, sweet smell filled the room, and the cookies we tested were delicious. I ate about six of them while Joan tucked some away herself, beaming. "It's so nice to see you really eat," she said.

"These are good." I grabbed another one, shaped like a star, and took a big bite.

"We still have to decorate them." She handed me some shakers of colored sugar. "And you have to tell me what else happened last night."

"Brian's girlfriend caught him kissing me," I said around the rest of my cookie. "And instead of sticking up for me, he acted like he'd made a big mistake. He dropped me like I was poison and started begging her to forgive him."

Joan's face crinkled into sympathy. "That's pretty rough," she said.

"He was supposed to walk me home, but he ditched me in the park instead." I shook way too much sugar on a cookie. "I mean, I ran off. But he could have followed me if he'd wanted."

She shook her head. "He sounds like bad news."

"I know, but . . . I like him."

"Why?" She started arranging cookies on a flowered ceramic plate. "What about that other boy you went out with, Tim?"

In my mind, I compared the two boys' kissing styles and how they'd made me feel. "There's just something about Brian," I said, feeling my face go hot.

She glanced at me and then back down at the plate. "Umm-hmm. Like sex appeal?"

Sex was one topic I did not want to discuss with Joan. "It's not just that," I said, truthfully. "Brian's deep. He understands things most kids don't." I didn't even know exactly what I meant. Brian understood about Dani, but not so much that he was nice to her. And he understood about parents who weren't perfect, but at least he got to live with his parents.

Still, it just seemed like he'd lived more and done more thinking than a lot of the silly kids at school, Tim included.

"I don't know, Rose. If he's really a good person, he'll make the right choices about his girlfriend and you. He won't keep stringing you both along. But I think you should date other boys."

A face appeared in the window of the back door, along with the sound of an urgent knock. It was Kimber.

Joan ushered her in, and she shrugged out of her coat and accepted a cookie and started talking in the space of about three seconds. "You won't believe what happened at school today! I had to come tell you!"

"What?" Joan and I said at the same time.

"Brian and Mara broke up!"

My heart started beating fast. "They did? How do you know?"

"Well, apparently," she said, "there was this big dramatic fight in the lunchroom. She was yelling at him and he wasn't answering and she—get this—threw her chocolate milk at him. She got sent to the office for it!"

Joan giggled and Kimber did too.

I didn't. I knew Brian hated a big scene.

Aside from sorry for him, I didn't know how to feel. Yeah, glad that he wasn't with Mara anymore. But it would've been nice if breaking up had been his idea, not hers.

Besides, would the breakup be for real? Mara was such a dramatic girl that she probably broke up with Brian on a weekly basis. Almost every time I'd seen them together, they'd been fighting. She'd stormed out of his newspaper meeting; she'd yelled at him last night.

But every time, he stayed to comfort her.

I watched Joan hold out our plate of cookies to Kimber and thought about what she'd said. It probably would be better to date other boys. Brian wasn't showing much character. It wasn't like he'd called to find out how I was doing today.

But I didn't want other boys. I wanted Brian.

"Guess what else," Kimber said, her cheeks glowing pink. "Leonard asked me out!"

"He did?" I squealed. "That's wonderful!"

"Where, when, and what are you doing?" Joan asked.

"That's the problem," Kimber said. "He wants to take me to the Science Center in Pittsburgh."

"Oh, no," Joan said.

"Uh-huh. The one place in the city my parents have taken me. Like, a hundred times."

"Did you tell him that?" I asked.

She shook her head. "How could I, when he was so proud of himself for thinking of it? And I mean, it *is* sweet. He's trying to appeal to my interests and all."

"I guess the Science Center could be romantic," Joan said, her voice doubtful. "It does have the IMAX theater. Maybe something scary will be playing, and you'll have to snuggle up close."

"I already thought of that," Kimber said glumly. "This month's show is *Bulldozers of the World.*"

"*Bulldozers?*"

Joan and I looked at each other and started laughing, and then Kimber laughed too.

Lee McClain

Joan held up a hand. "This reminds me of something," she said, still chuckling. "Michelle had this boyfriend once who took her riding on his uncle's backhoe," she said. "That was the whole date! She said he tried to kiss her while he was revving the motor, but he pushed the wrong button and it started going backwards. They ended up in a ditch."

"Maybe heavy machinery is a turn-on for guys," I said, still giggling.

"Not for me," Kimber grabbed another cookie. "It figures: I finally get a date, and he's taking me to the Science Center."

"There are a lot of cute restaurants on the North Side," Joan said. "Maybe this is a blessing in disguise. Your parents will feel comfortable, and you'll feel comfortable, and you can steer him toward . . . what was the name of that little Thai place?" She got up and started hunting through her big jar of matchbooks. "Wait, I'll find it."

There was a loud knock on the front door. Was it Brian? Had he come at last to check on me?

Kimber must have had the same thought, because she ran over to peek out the living room window. And then she turned to Joan and me in the doorway.

"It's the police," she said.

Chapter Eleven

All the cops I'd ever known came rising out of my past to haunt me. I shrank back against the living room wall as panicky memories sparked through my mind.

Where was Dani? Where was Mom? And how could I keep the cops from coming in and seeing them?

Only half aware that I was having a flashback, that Mom and Dani weren't here, I stiffened and prepared to protect my family.

But Joan was way ahead of me. She marched to the door and flung it open.

"Hi there. How can I help you?"

"Is there a Rose Graham here? Foster child?"

"Yes." Joan didn't move.

I cringed. Joan was so naïve. If she didn't start acting all respectful, she was just going to make things worse.

"We need to talk with her, ma'am."

"About what?" Joan still blocked the doorway. The pleasant smile was gone from her face.

I couldn't help liking the feeling of being protected.

"They might be here about the computer equipment at the paper," Kimber stage-whispered to me.

"What?"

Kimber's words had made me miss the latest lines between Joan and the officers. Now she was ushering them in. "You can talk with Rose," she was saying, "if you treat her with respect."

The two officers introduced themselves to me, but I was so nervous that I immediately forgot their names. One, the woman, was as blond and hard-looking as some of the women who'd used to hang around near our apartment. The other, a tall, skinny black guy, had a friendlier smile. But I didn't trust him, either.

"Sit down, Rose," he said.

"We have a few questions to ask you about some computer equipment that's gone missing at your school," said the lady.

Kimber snapped her fingers. "I knew it!"

The black guy flicked open a pad of paper. "And you are . . ." he said to Kimber.

She blushed and gave her name.

"You know something about this equipment?" he asked.

"Just that it's missing," she said. "It was all over school."

"Mmm-hmm." He shot a glance at me and I looked away. I knew I was acting guilty, but cops always made me nervous.

"Excuse me, but why are you here?" Joan asked.

The blond officer jerked her head toward me. "Her name came up in connection with the theft," she said.

"Why? Because I'm a foster kid?" I blurted out.

"That shouldn't have anything to do with it," Joan said.

The black officer chuckled. "Oh, yes. Always the first to be accused and the last exonerated."

We all looked at him, surprised.

He leaned toward me. "I grew up in the system too," he said in a low voice. "Don't worry. I'll be fair to you."

"You were reported seen in the vicinity of the school last night," the blonde said. "That's when the theft took place."

"Rose was visiting another family last night," Joan said.

The blond officer took the name of Brian's family, and the two cops glanced at each other. Either they knew the family or they'd questioned Brian already.

"Did you pick her up from the house?" the black cop asked Joan.

"No," she said, frowning. "She walked home."

"What time did she arrive?"

I was sweating. Of course Joan knew the exact time—ten o'clock—and of course, being an honest type, she said it.

"And you left your friends' house at—" He looked at me.

"Remember, honey, we'll check it all out," the blonde said, like she was sure I'd lie.

"I left around seven," I admitted. "Or seven-thirty. I didn't look at my watch."

The officers glanced at each other again. "And so from seven or seven-thirty until ten, you were walking home?" the guy asked. For the first time, his voice was skeptical.

"Um . . ." I looked at Joan.

Her gaze on me was warm and steady. "Tell them who you were with," she said.

So, for the second time, I explained that I'd been with Brian on the playground.

"Did he bring you back here?"

I sighed and shook my head. "No, we had an argument and I left the playground. I walked around for about an hour before I came home."

"Anyone see you?"

I stared down at the red-and-blue throw rug, straightening its fringed edge with my toe. "I tried to stay out of sight. I was upset."

"Too bad," said the blonde. I couldn't tell how she meant it.

"Did you go onto school property?" asked the other cop.

"No. I just walked." And cried, but he didn't need to know that.

They looked at each other, nodded, and stood. "We'll be back in touch," the woman said, and they walked out the front door.

"They think I did it," I moaned as soon as they left. "I'm doomed. Mom's never gonna want us back if everyone thinks I'm still a criminal!"

"Still?" Kimber asked, wide-eyed.

Joan came up behind me and straightened my shoulders. "You aren't a criminal and you never were. You did what you had to do and I'm proud of you for that. And I won't let you be convicted of a crime you didn't commit."

"You believe I didn't do it?" I asked her, honestly surprised. She had no particular reason to trust me, and she knew my history.

"Of course," she said.

"You?" I asked Kimber.

"Uh-huh," she said. "And I have an idea of who gave your name to the police, too."

She and Joan looked at each other and then spoke at the same time. "Mara."

That night, I sat down at the computer. But instead of logging onto ALTLIVES as usual, I created a new file and started drafting my next

"Alien View" column. I called it "Foster Teens: Number One Aliens."

After a couple of false starts, words poured out of me. I wrote about being separated from my family and home and everything familiar. About coming to a new town and trying to fit in. About how I'd been the automatic suspect when there was a theft at the paper, and how that felt.

"Being an outsider can make you strong," I finished, "but it's a lonely life."

I saved the draft and e-mailed it to my school account. I wanted to polish it before sending it to Brian for editing. Even though I was mad at him, I didn't want to give him bad work.

But the next day at the newspaper office, I found out that Brian nit-picking my grammar was the least of my worries.

I hadn't wanted to go to school, but Joan made me. She also called Kimber and told her to come walk with me so that I wouldn't be alone.

That was why Kimber wound up at the newspaper office too, and when we walked in, about five of the staff were there. Including Tim and Leonard. And Mara. And Brian.

But they weren't typing or doing layout at the computers. They were sorting stacks of paper and cleaning the walls.

"Hi," I said tentatively to these people who'd started to seem like my friends—excepting Mara, of course.

Nobody answered. Nobody even looked at me.

I glanced around the office and my eyes widened. Papers spilled out of open file drawers and framed award certificates lay on the floor, their glass fronts cracked. The laptops were missing from the center table.

"What happened in here?" I asked, shocked. I'd known about the theft, but the vandalism spoke to a kind of anger I wasn't prepared for.

Mara shot me a scornful look. "Don't play dumb," she said. "We know you did all this. And swiped the laptops and erased the hard drives. There's no way we can do an issue now."

"How could you do it, Rose?" Brian asked, his voice heavy with discouragement. "I know you were mad at me, but this affects the whole student body."

"Yeah, especially us," said Tim, looking glum. "I had everything laid out, and now it's gone. Thanks a lot."

I guess we could safely say he was over his crush on me!

"And our entire archive, gone," Leonard said, waving toward the overflowing file cabinet.

Kimber marched over to him. "You're blaming Rose for that? You're crazy."

I lifted my hands, palms up. "I didn't do it, guys."

"Yeah, right," Brian said.

I focused on him; his lack of belief in me hurt the most. "How can you think I'd do something so awful?"

He met my eyes. "Mom told me you've stolen before."

My cheeks flamed hot. "Yeah, when my family was starving," I said. "That's a little different from trashing a newspaper office and stealing from friends I care about."

"Stealing can get to be a habit," Brian said.

"So can judging people based on their backgrounds," I snapped back.

Leonard stepped toward Kimber. "Maybe we jumped to conclusions," he said slowly.

"Maybe, genius." Kimber rolled her eyes at him. But her lips quirked upward into a smile.

The way they looked at each other made me ache inside. I'd hoped for that kind of closeness with Brian.

And I appreciated Leonard standing up for me, but would he have done it if he wasn't three-quarters in love with Kimber?

"Come on, Rose." Kimber took my arm and tugged me toward the door. "If these are your friends, you need some new ones. Besides," she added, glaring at Mara, "I have an idea of what really went down the other night."

* * *

During my free period, I went to the computer lab. First I sent Brian an e-mail. For the subject line, I typed, "Guilty until proven inno-cent??????" In the message box I wrote, "Think about who really has a motive for trashing the newspaper office and blaming me." I attached the column I'd written last night without bother-ing to proof it—he didn't deserve the courtesy—and hit "send."

Next, I logged onto ALTLIVES for my daily dose of family. I was too mad at Brian—and at his mom, who'd revealed my past to him—to check on Dani first as usual. Instead I went right to Mom.

And got a surprising new message. The word "Congratulations!" flashed big across the screen, and beneath it: "You have logged enough hours for the ALTLIVES Switch."

Immediately the video came on, and I saw Mom in her room, hand over her forehead in a twitchy, half asleep state.

It surprised me because lately she'd been up and about a lot more. At first she'd just talked to neighbors in the hall, but the last couple of times I'd logged on, she'd been taking the bus to a red brick building a couple of miles away.

Now it looked like she had gone back to her old sleepy self.

The door of Mom's bedroom opened, and my heart started pounding double time. Had someone broken in? Or, against all odds, had Mom made a friend?

But when I saw who was at the door, I really freaked.

It was me.

But it was me the way I used to be: my clothes all baggy, hair greasy and pulled back in a pony-tail, face twisted with anxiety. Just looking at my-self made me feel almost sick, remembering.

Was the machine stuck in the past? Had it somehow been videotaping us before Dani and I had come to live in Linden Falls?

On the screen, I watched Dani push through the door behind me, and we both sat on Mom's bed, trying to rouse her. She turned her back on us and I went around to get up in her face, my own expression frustrated. Eventually I started yelling at her, and Dani cried, and Mom sat up and yelled back.

That gave me the creeps, because I knew I'd never yelled at my mom like that.

So where was this scene coming from?

I watched myself slam out of the room and the apartment and go down the stairs. I already knew what my double was going to do: steal. I could tell from the sick, scared look on my face. Man, no wonder I got caught!

I tore my eyes away from the computer screen and took a quick glance around the lab. If any-one saw what was onscreen, I was cooked. It would be the evidence everyone at Linden High needed to hang, draw, and quarter me. But luckily, the lab was almost deserted and no one appeared interested in me and my work.

To my surprise, my on-screen self didn't leave the apartment building. Instead, I went to the third floor, looked around to make sure I was alone, found Mrs. Reynolds's hidden key, and opened her apartment door. Inside, I went straight to her cookie jar and pulled out the two twenties hidden there. I grabbed a loaf of bread and a package of American cheese from her refrigerator. I was reaching for something else, but then I pulled back, looking scared, and darted out of the apartment as a door from the back of the place opened. I caught a glimpse of Mrs. Reynolds, her face angry, before the camera pulled out into the hallway.

I looked away from the screen as shame flooded my body. Stealing from Mrs. Reynolds? That was low. She'd always been kind to Dani and me, had invited us often for soup and toast and grandmotherly care. That was how I knew where her spare key and her money were hidden. She'd been open and trusting with us.

When I looked back at the screen, there was a little box on it: *ALTLIFE! Do you choose to switch over?* There was a space to check off "yes" or "no"—and a clock counting down from five minutes.

Was this the dangerous decision Fred had warned me about at the beginning? I was starting to understand but I had to make sure. "Switch over to what?" I typed.

Instead of telling me, a smaller box with its own video came into the corner of the screen. It showed the day I'd gotten arrested for shoplifting, the day that had started this whole spiral into foster care and Linden Falls. I was in the grocery store, stuffing lunch meat packages into my coat pockets.

My heart thumped as I remembered, and I could hardly watch as the moment of my arrest came closer. If only I hadn't grabbed the candy bar for Dani on the way out, I wouldn't have been caught.

I watched myself approach the store's exit. Watched my hand snake toward the candy bars.

Then, without taking anything, I pulled my hand back and walked out of the store, free and clear.

The little video box closed and I was back to the scene at my old apartment, fixing sandwiches in the kitchen, with the message box at the top of the screen.

The onscreen clock was down to 1:59.

Full understanding dawned, fighting with a sense of logical disbelief. The ALTLIVES game was giving me the chance to turn back time, to go back home and live with Mom and Dani like we had before Social Services came in.

I'd known the game was weird, but I'd gotten used to it, had stopped wondering how it happened that the computer could go wherever it wanted, see and hear around corners, and generally invade people's lives.

This was beyond weird, though. This was magic, supernatural, paranormal. It was like a fairy tale coming true, an alternate reality. If I hadn't stolen the candy bar and gotten caught, this was what my life would be.

It was what I wanted, what I'd been working so hard to get. I should have been jumping for joy. And yet, my hand hovering on the mouse, I hesitated.

I didn't like the self I saw on-screen. I didn't want to be a person who yelled at Mom and stole from Mrs. Reynolds.

And even though my so-called normal life really sucked right now, it gave me space to think about me and my future and what I wanted. I wasn't just struggling to survive anymore. I'd made friends, even though most of them were mad at me right now. Joan's house had started to seem like a refuge.

And yet I knew it was better for our family to be together.

Why did I have to decide something so hard?

On the screen, I watched Dani come into the kitchen. She grabbed slices of the bread and cheese I'd stolen and stuffed them into her mouth. Not only was she obviously hungry, but she looked like a stray dog, dirty and mindless.

A big part of me hated The Witch, but when I pictured the last time I'd seen Dani, all cute and fresh-faced in her Gap clothes, carefully carrying dishes to the dishwasher, I knew she was better off there.

The clock was down to the last fifteen seconds. I fought with myself. I hated how powerless I felt, now that I knew custody of us was all about Mom's decision and Mom's behavior. I had no control.

The game had just given me a way to regain control. But the price was high for me and higher still for Dani.

With one second to go, I clicked "no."

The screen went black.

I sank back in my rolling chair as the computer lab around me came back into focus. I felt like I'd been running marathons through my old world. Being here, in this orderly, organized place with clear rules and adults in charge, felt like a relief, like I'd awakened from a nightmare.

I knew I'd made the right decision. I didn't want to be the girl I'd seen on-screen, and I wanted more for Dani and Mom than sickness and hunger and hopelessness.

Was that the way Mom had felt when she'd given us up into foster care? Had she done it out of loving us?

But even though I knew I'd made the right decision, and even though I could understand her decision a little better, I felt like crying. Was I giving up on our family, then? Was I as bad as Mom? Had I just made the decision for Dani and I to continue on in Linden Falls—in our separate families—while Mom lived alone in that dark apartment?

No.

That wasn't right, either.

Up until now, I hadn't pressed about visiting Mom. I'd accepted what Fred had initially told me—that until she got herself together, it was better if we didn't visit.

Besides, all my energy had gone to staying close to Dani. And, of course, I'd had ALTLIVES.

Now, I began to see that I'd been wrong to rely on a computer as my reality. I needed to show Mom how we'd changed in real life, how well Dani could do if properly cared for. Then she'd want us. And she'd be motivated to do whatever it took to get us back.

I could push Fred to get us visitation rights, but that would take forever. If I wanted to give our family a chance, I had to act.

Right now.

Chapter Twelve

Luckily, it was an unseasonably warm night and all the kids at Brian's house were playing outside.

Unluckily, The Witch was with them.

I crouched behind some bushes, looking for my chance. After a few minutes, Dani drifted over to my side of the driveway while The Witch was busy teaching one of the other kids to ride a tricycle on the sidewalk.

"Dani!" I hissed. "It's Rose."

Her head lifted and she smiled, and I felt an incredible rush of love for her. She was so adorable, with her hair in neat ponytails, a few freckles on her nose from playing outside, wearing blue overalls and a flowered turtleneck. I felt proud that she was my sister.

And how could Mom not want to do anything in her power to get such a great kid back?

"Dani, come over and stand by the car, but don't look at me."

"We play a game?" she asked as she walked in my direction, still smiling. "Where you hide, Rose?"

"Over here," I said, popping my head out from behind the bush, "but don't look at me. Pretend you're looking at the car."

Amazingly, she did what I said.

I had to talk fast, with one eye on The Witch. "Dani, we're going to go on a little trip," I said.

"Right now?"

"In a couple minutes."

She squatted down by the bush, forgetting my directive not to look at me. "It almost time for bed."

"How about staying up late tonight?"

"Why?"

"So we can go on a trip," I said. "So we can go see Mom."

"But Mom right there." She pointed down the driveway toward The Witch.

I took a deep breath. "I mean our real mom, Dani. Back home. In our apartment."

She stood up. "I no want to." And she turned as if she was about to walk away.

"Wait!" I reached out and grabbed her leg. "Stay here. Talk to me." I thought fast. If Dani didn't want to go, it was a disaster. At the same time, it reminded me just how important it was to get our family back together *now*. Dani didn't have the memory capacity to keep our real family in her mind. Plus she was getting too attached here.

"Dani," I said, "remember how you like riding on the bus?"

"Yeah!" she yelled.

"Sssh!"

She started doing the hand movements for "The Wheels on the Bus" and singing in her loud, tone-deaf way.

"Do you want to go for a real bus ride?" I interrupted.

"Um, sure!" She started to crawl into the bushes with me, thinking we were pretending.

From the bottom of the driveway, The Witch clapped her hands. "Okay, kids, listen up! I want everyone upstairs and in pajamas right now! I'll be upstairs to check on you in ten minutes. Hustle!"

That played right into my plan. "Just put your pajama top on over your clothes," I told Dani. "Get in bed, and after she's come in to kiss you goodnight, I'll come get you."

She looked scared.

"Go on," I said, smiling at her. "It'll be a lot of fun. A real bus!"

"Okay!" She ran toward the house.

I backed out of the bushes—and felt two hands clamp down on my upper arms.

My heart raced out of control.

"What are you, crazy?" snarled a voice in my ear.

Brian.

His grip on my arms stayed tight. I sagged back against him, my heart racing.

"It's bad enough for you to run away your-self," he continued. "But you can't sneak off at night with Dani. That's completely crazy. How are you going to travel, in a furniture truck?"

"No." I twisted away and looked at him. "There's a bus leaving Linden Falls at nine o'clock. And since you're here, you can help me get Dani out of the house."

"No way," he said. "I'm completely against this."

"Why do you care?" I asked. "You just think I'm a criminal."

"I read your column," he said, his voice gruff. "I might have misjudged you."

A voice came from the back steps of his house. "Brian? Is that you?"

It was his mom.

"Yeah. I'm, um, on my phone."

"Well, hurry up. I need you to get the kids in bed." The back door slammed.

My curiosity won over my nerves. "Why does she need you to do that? I thought you hated the little kids."

"I don't hate them," he said. "They just drive me crazy."

"But you put them to bed anyway?"

"I lift them into bed," he explained. "Two are in cribs, and Dani and Micah have bed rails that are hard to put up and down. And Mom has a bad back."

"You do that every night?"

"Dad's gone a lot." He looked embarrassed, like I was going to make fun of him for helping.

Instead, I kissed him.

His lips felt firm and moist and really, really sexy. I could have gotten lost there, but I forced my brain back to my plan.

Pulling away, I looked into his dazed face. "Brian," I said, "you have to help me."

"How?"

"Sneak Dani out without anyone knowing. Bring her down here to me, and I'll take the heat for it."

Right away, he started shaking his head. "No. Uh-uh. You can't get me to do something crazy just by kissing me."

"That's not why I kissed you."

"I'd do better to go tell Mom what you're planning right now," he said. "Rose, long-distance buses are full of crazy people. You're headed for the inner city, and you'll get there late at night. Have you even thought about the risks?"

I knew he was right. But I also knew that there was a bigger risk to my soul and to Dani's if we didn't try to make it as a family.

"I have to do this, Brian," I tried to explain. "It means everything to me. Like you quit sports to work on the newspaper, that drive you have. My drive is to get my family back together, and this is about my last chance to do it." I paused. "You know how much you love your dad, even though he's not the best dad in the world? That's how I feel about Mom. And she needs us right now."

He studied me for a minute, his forehead wrinkled into a frown. "All right, look. You stay here. I'll see what I can do."

"You'll get Dani?"

"I'll see what I can do, and I'll come back out and tell you."

It was my best shot at success, so I waited.

And waited.

And waited.

Just when I thought I was going to freeze, just when I was ready to start in there myself so we wouldn't miss the bus, he came outside.

And he had Dani with him. My hero!

He was frowning, but he held up some jingling car keys. "Look, I'm taking you guys home myself," he said. "But if it's not safe, I'm not letting you stay."

I threw my arms around him. "How'd you get the car?"

"Don't ask." He herded us into the old beater car that sat parked in the garage, Dani in back and me in front.

We didn't talk much on the hour-long drive into the city. Brian was clearly doing this against his better judgment. Dani fell asleep in the backseat.

As for me, I was half exhilarated and half sick with anticipation and fear.

I'd gotten Dani and myself this far. We were ready to convince Mom to work hard and become a real mother to us. We had to do it in one night; that was all the time we had before Joan and The Witch discovered we were missing.

But could we do in one night what we hadn't been able to do in the years leading up to it?

By the time we knocked on our old apartment door, my palms were damp and my stomach tied in knots. It was ten o'clock. Brian had carried Dani upstairs and she was still half asleep in his arms.

I knocked again and looked around the familiar hallway. Same brown stain in the gray industrial-style carpet. Same cold draft from the cracked window at the end of the hall. Same sour smell of everyone's dinner.

The door opened.

And there was Mom.

She wore her old robe, blue terrycloth, belted around her skinny middle. Her hair hung down over her shoulders and her eyes had dark circles under them. She looked tired, but her eyes were wide open; I could tell she hadn't been sleeping.

Feelings flooded over me like a storm, crazy and chaotic. I wanted to hug her. Wanted her to hug me. Knew she might cringe away; wanted to protect her from being overwhelmed.

Dani's feelings were simpler. "Mommy!" she cried and struggled away from Brian to run and wrap her arms around Mom's waist.

Mom stared down at Dani. Her fingers went to Dani's pigtails and she stroked them, carefully.

Then she looked at me. "What are you doing here?"

Her voice sounded rusty, like she hadn't been using it much.

I cleared my throat. "We wanted to see you. Can we come in?"

Mom didn't move from the doorway. In fairness, she might not have been able to move with Dani clinging to her.

Still, it didn't exactly feel welcoming.

"Who's that?" she asked, nodding at Brian.

"He's my friend," I said.

"He's my new brother," Dani added.

Mom drew in her breath. "Come inside," she said.

"Thanks," I said to Brian, suddenly wanting him to leave. I'd been so worried about getting here that I hadn't thought about how it would all appear to him.

Now I contrasted my home with his and felt ashamed. What would he think of me when he saw the mess the apartment was sure to be? What did he already think?

"I'd like to come in with you," he said quietly. "Make sure you're okay."

"We're fine."

"Just for a minute," he insisted. Then he put his hand on my back and guided me into the apartment.

It seemed a lot smaller than when we'd lived here. The furniture looked shabbier, and the dust on the end table embarrassed me.

Dani ran around looking at the world that was all she'd known for most of her eight years. "Where all the toys?" she asked.

Mom didn't say anything, just took Dani's hand and led her to the corner of the room. There was the single doll Dani had loved half to death, neatly bundled in a baby blanket and tucked into a little box.

Mom's eyes filled. "I've kept it there for you," she said, her voice rising in a little sob.

I got a little teary too, but my heart soared. She did want us back!

Mom and I might have been all emotional, but Dani wasn't. Or if she was, she didn't express it in the same way. "I want more toys!" she yelled.

Mom bit her lip as she watched Dani. Then she turned to me. "Is he staying?" she asked without looking at Brian.

"No."

"Okay." Mom looked relieved.

"Let's go out in the hall," I said to Brian as Dani continued to whine.

It was like we were on the same wavelength as we moved out of the circle of light cast by the bare bulb. He took hold of my upper arms and for a minute I thought he was going to kiss me, but when Mom yelled inside the apartment, his face twisted into concern. "Should we go help calm Dani down?"

"I think you should go home." That was hard for me to say, because a part of me really wanted Brian to stay. Not just because I loved the way his hands felt on my arms, but because I was scared to be here alone with Mom and Dani.

Figure that: scared! Scared of what I'd had my whole life; scared of what I'd been fighting for ever since I moved to Linden Falls. But now, faced with the reality, I saw how protective Linden Falls had been for me. How I could have trusted Joan or The Witch with Dani while I talked to a boy, but I was nervous and scared about what my own mother might do. Not that she'd hurt Dani, but that she'd completely fall apart.

"I want to stay," he said. "Make sure you guys are okay." Inside the apartment, Mom's abrupt shout and Dani's crying punctuated his words.

"You're making her nervous. She's not used to strangers."

"Is she stable?"

"Yes," I said, though I wasn't at all sure of that. Mom seemed different from when we'd left. She was up and about and nervous instead of depressed and sleepy.

But I had what I wanted, I had my dream, and the only way to find out if it would work was to go ahead and live it. "We're fine," I said. "Just go."

"You have my cell phone number," he said. "Call when you're ready to come home."

Tears pushed at the backs of my eyes. Where was home?

"Come here." He pulled me to him in a hug, then cupped a hand behind my head and kissed me.

Maybe it was because I was so upset and scared, but that kiss was the most intense yet. It took me away from the dirty, stale-smelling hall-way and into a fantasy world of warmth and light and love.

He lifted his head, gathered me tighter into his arms and just held me.

Tenderness and caring filled the strong arms that wrapped around me. I rested my head against his broad shoulder and let my mind go blank for a minute, let myself just rest and dream of someday finding a comfort like this that would truly last.

It felt like heaven. Just too good.

Finally he lifted his head and looked hard into my eyes. "Call me," he said.

Then he turned and strode down the hall.

I watched him go. And then I went back into the apartment where Dani cried and Mom stood silent.

Chapter Thirteen

I remember reading a story once about a couple of people making polite small talk, never mentioning the giant elephant—or was it a gorilla?—that sat in the middle of the room.

That was me and Mom.

We got Dani calmed down by plunking her in front of some junky music show. And then we alternated between watching it with her and talking.

We talked about the neighbors. About Dani's new ability to tie her own shoes. About how rainy it had been lately.

We didn't talk about the giant fact of Mom giving us up into foster care.

I should have been happy because I had what I wanted. My family was together, safe and warm, even eating tortilla chips Mom had bought herself at the grocery store.

Instead, I felt like I was going crazy. And from the way Mom kept rubbing her hands together like she was washing them, I guessed she was going crazy too.

"Let's leave," I said.

"What?"

"Let's get out of here." I stood up. "If we stay we might get in trouble, since this visit is kind of off the books. Wouldn't it be fun to go somewhere together? I mean, since you're getting out again and all." I flushed, somehow embarrassed to refer to the time when she'd stayed in bed for a year.

"Is that what you really want, Rose?" She studied my face. "For us to go somewhere?"

No! I wanted to scream. *I want us to be a normal family in a normal place! I want you to convince a judge that you're normal, so you can take care of us in a normal way!*

But how could you say that to your mentally ill mother?

Before I could make up an answer, Mom stood. "All right," she said. "Let's get out of here tonight."

I stared at her. "Really?"

"Come on," she said. "We don't have much time." She started walking around pulling things together: a coat, a purse, even a suitcase I didn't know we had.

I'd been thinking of a trip to the all-night Wal-Mart or something, but Mom seemed to have something else in mind.

Her unusual actions got Dani's attention. "What Mommy do?" she asked me, and I knew why.

For the past couple of years, we'd only seen Mom move in low gear: creeping around the apartment, lying in bed, talking in a low voice. It was bizarre to see her fast, jerky movements now.

So bizarre that I blurted out a question. "What happened to you, Mom?" I asked. "Did you get counseling?"

"I'm seeing a counselor and I'm on medication," she said. "They haven't got the meds quite adjusted yet, but you can see I have a lot more energy."

"That's great." It was scary, too. She seemed so different. "Um, where are we going, exactly?"

"We'll go stay with my old friend Justine in Philly. We've been in touch. There might be a job."

Mom working in a job?

Philadelphia? Tonight?

I was already having second thoughts. "What about school for us?" I asked. "What about when Social Services finds out we ran away?"

She waved her hand. "You are such a worrier!" she said. "Relax. We're a family again!" She ruffled my hair and gave Dani a big kiss on the top of her head, making her giggle.

It was what I'd dreamed of: Mom wanted us, and was taking charge, being a real parent.

Yet it wasn't so easy to turn off the worrying. "What about train tickets? And we'll need food. Doesn't it take a whole day to get to Philly on the train?"

I was thinking, too, about Joan and The Witch. How frantic they'd be when they discovered our empty beds. How they'd think we'd been abducted and start a search.

And what kind of trouble would Brian get in?

Still, I argued with myself, that could all blow over.

"We'll stop at Giant Eagle on the way to the station," she said. "It's open all night."

It seemed a little crazy to leave at eleven o'clock at night. But I wasn't tired, and from the looks of it, neither was Dani. And Mom definitely had energy to spare.

On the way to the store in the misty rain, we all held hands and Mom asked about our lives in Linden Falls. I told her how I was getting good grades and writing for the newspaper, and she smiled. "You've always been smart, Rose. It doesn't surprise me that you're doing well."

Her approval poured into an empty place inside me. She'd relied on me, but never said I was doing a good job.

"I go school, too!" Dani bragged. "And I make cookies and help Mom at home."

Dani went on talking while I shot a look at Mom's face. How did it feel to have her daughter call another woman "Mom"?

Not that good, I guessed. She gripped Dani's hand and walked faster, to the point where Dani started to whine and protest.

As soon as we entered the store, Dani went wild. She ran from one end of the produce aisle to the other, grabbing vegetables and fruit, singing something crazy at top volume. The few other shoppers stared at her, then at Mom and me.

I looked at Mom. She cringed, her head retracting into her shoulders like a turtle's. Her eyes blinked as if the store's bright light hurt them.

Nerves twisted my stomach. Controlling Dani was going to be up to me.

I ran to her and put my arms around her. "Dani, slow down! Let's put the vegetables back where they belong. We'll make a game of it!"

That worked to get us through the produce aisle, but once we hit cereal we were in trouble again. "Sugar Bears!" Dani screamed, and before I could stop her, she'd ripped open the box.

I grabbed it from her and she threw herself down on the floor. "Mine, mine!" she yelled, kicking her legs.

"We've got to get through here fast," I told Mom. "Where's the cart?"

"I didn't get one," she said, looking like she wanted to be anywhere else but here. "Let's just go to the train station, okay? We can buy food on the train."

I hated to question her judgment, but it looked like I was the more practical of the two of us. "How much money do you have, anyway?"

Right there in the store, she opened her purse and pulled out a wad. It looked like tons of money, but when I counted it, there was $120—mostly in small bills.

It was a lot, and then again it wasn't. I doubted it would buy us all train tickets.

Dani lay across the aisle, kicking and sobbing, blocking the path of an old man who wanted to get through. I tried to move her to one side, wincing when she struck my hands away. The old man snorted with disgust and turned his cart around.

I squatted there, stroking Dani's head, thinking while I murmured for her to calm down. It was really no wonder she was having a tantrum. It was way past her bedtime, and she'd been ripped—by me—out of a comfortable home. Being with Mom had to confuse her. My own mixed feelings had me tied up in knots, and Dani didn't have the capacity to understand what was going on.

My mistake. I never should have agreed to start a trip this late at night.

Or *was* it my mistake? I glanced up at Mom. She was rubbing her hands together again like she was washing them, studying the labels on cereal boxes.

I thought of Kimber, who'd been amazed I'd taken care of a Down's syndrome sister for so long by myself. I thought of Joan, who would have swept in and gushed and taken over.

I thought of The Witch, who would have put Dani in the time-out chair.

Dani was winding down now, crying quietly and reaching her arms up for me to hold her. I picked her up and reeled backwards against the shelves. She'd gotten bigger in Linden Falls.

"Look," I said to Mom, "why don't you go sit with her in the tables by the deli. Get her a cookie or something. I'll call the station and make sure we have enough money for tickets."

Mom looked uncertain, so I guided her over to the tables, my arms aching from carrying Dani. I went to the counter and got Dani a cookie and brought it back. And then I walked toward the front of the store.

As I got change and looked up the number of the train station, I was thinking.

There was no question Mom was better. A couple of months ago she wouldn't have left the apartment. Now she was in a grocery store, talking about getting a job, back in touch with an old friend.

Still, she wasn't taking care of us the way a

parent should. If we made it to Philadelphia it was going to be my job to hold everything together: to keep Dani happy, to hide us from Social Services, and to figure out how to get food and find an apartment.

I could probably do it, but I wasn't sure I wanted to. I'd had a taste of life as a normal teen, I'd made friends, I'd done okay for myself.

Part of me just wanted to go back, to entrust Dani to The Witch, to listen to Joan and Dale fussing over me.

I knew things wouldn't be perfect in Linden Falls. The police thought I'd stolen the computer equipment, and my running away just made me look more like a criminal.

But the alternative was to get Mom and Dani on a train to Philly—far from Brian and my new normal life.

Calling Brian now would mean facing the mess I'd left in Linden Falls. It would mean giving up, maybe forever, on Mom and Dani and me being a family.

But it was the best of the two alternatives, and more than that, it felt like the right thing to do. I fed coins into the pay phone and started punching in Brian's number.

And then Dani ran by heading toward the store's exit. Mom was nowhere in sight.

"Dani, wait!" I dropped the phone and ran after her.

She ignored me, jumped on the floor mats to open the doors, and ran out into the dark, rainy parking lot.

I glanced back to see Mom plodding—not running, not even walking fast—in our general direction. And then I sprinted out after Dani.

She was easy to see, because headlights illuminated her.

Headlights from a big van speeding her way.

"Dani!" I screamed and ran, running faster than I'd ever run in my life but feeling like it was slow motion. "Dani, look out!"

Cold rain dripped into my eyes. I heard screams and screeching brakes.

And then everything blurred together as I slammed into Dani, rolled with her out of the van's path, and bit down hard on my tongue, tasting blood.

I tried to sit up, crying now, feeling Dani's damp limbs for injuries. Something felt like it was crushing my foot.

"Back the van up!" someone yelled.

"Are you okay?" I screamed at Dani.

"Why you push me?" she said, sobbing. "You give me an ouchie!" She held out a scraped arm.

I kissed it, inspected her again, and breathed a huge sigh of relief, though the tears wouldn't stop coming. She was okay.

Voices and lights made me look up, and I realized there was a circle of people surrounding us.

And there was a familiar voice. "Let me through. Those are my girls!"

Mom.

"Are you all right?" she asked, kneeling down beside us.

I drew in a breath, ready to say we were fine, when something exploded inside me. "No, we're not all right," I shouted at her. "Why couldn't you control her? She almost got killed!"

Mom pulled her head back in that turtle way she had.

Everything I'd been feeling came rushing out of me. "Why can't you be a normal mother? Why didn't you get more help for Dani? Why didn't you . . ." I gulped and gasped and swallowed. "Why didn't you show me I could be pretty?"

She looked surprised, head cocked to one side, eyes wide. "I . . . I don't know," she said, as if she was really thinking about it.

I held Dani tighter and sobbed.

The sound of a siren came closer and people started moving around. "That foot's going to need some medical attention," someone said.

"Who saw what happened?"

"That little girl ran out right in front of me. I didn't see her!"

"You were going too damn fast."

I shut out the bickering voices and let the world shrink back down to me, Mom, and Dani.

Dani reached up and touched my face. "I sorry, Rose," she said. "Don't cry."

"I'm sorry too," I said. And I was. Sorry for bringing her here. Sorry for making her hope even for a minute that we could be a normal family.

Sorry I'd yelled at Mom, ruining forever any chance she'd want us back.

An EMT guy did something to my shoe, which was good, because my foot was really starting to hurt. Another medical worker started checking Dani.

Mom knelt down on the wet asphalt and took my hand. "I'm so sorry, Rose. I want us to be together as a family, but I'm not ready yet."

I looked into her eyes. "Do you really want us?"

She nodded. "More than anything. Enough to"—she paused and took a deep breath—"enough to go out of the house to a therapy group every day. Can you believe it?"

I shook my head.

"You deserve a better life than I can give you right now," she said. "You deserve to be a normal teenager. And you're doing just fine at it, from what you've told me."

I let my breath out in a sigh. "Can I make a phone call?" I asked the EMT guy.

Because the person I wanted to talk to was Brian.

Chapter Fourteen

The group assembled around The Witch's kitchen table the next day wasn't anyone's idea of a good mix.

Joan. The Witch, of course. Me. My social worker Fred. And Brian, who'd insisted on sitting in.

Dani came and went. Depressingly enough, she seemed happy to be back in the place she now considered home.

The meeting, according to Fred, was supposed to help us all process what had happened. It was information that would be useful in our custody hearing, due in a couple of weeks.

Last night, as soon as I'd called Brian, everything kind of blurred. There was a trip to the hospital in an ambulance, a cast on my foot, and a lot of fussing and crying between me, Mom, Dani, and eventually Joan and The Witch. Pretty soon we all realized it wasn't doing any good to try and work things out there, and somehow everyone got home.

Fred cleared his throat as The Witch poured coffee for the adults. "Since this is the second runaway attempt," he said, "we probably need to reassess the custody arrangements for Rose and Dani."

Joan squeezed my hand under the table. "Let's not forget that Rose called Brian for help," she said in her ever perky way. "She could have remained with her mother, and left town."

I stared at the table in front of me. I couldn't have stayed with Mom; I knew that now.

"But let's also remember that she abducted Dani out of our house without permission and put her at risk," The Witch said.

I slouched lower in my seat.

"With the help of your son," Joan snapped.

"I'm well aware of that."

"The runaway efforts speak to the strong desire this family has to be together," Fred said. "That's why I think planning for some change in the custody arrangements is warranted."

Now was the time to express the only idea I'd had as I'd tossed and turned in my bed last night. It wasn't a good idea, but it was a way Dani and I could be together. I took a deep breath. "Maybe you could take me in," I said to The Witch. "As a foster kid, you know? I could help you with Dani and the other kids. Other than that, I'd stay out of your way."

Beside me, Joan let out a shuddery little sigh, but for once she didn't say anything.

Oh, great. Now I'd hurt the feelings of the only person at the table who was on my side. "Sorry," I whispered to her.

I shot a glance at The Witch. She opened her mouth and then closed it again.

Brian let out a harsh laugh. "Don't even think about it, Rose. You're too normal for this family."

All eyes turned to him.

"What does that mean?" The Witch asked.

"Oh, just that ever since Micah was born, you only care about retarded kids around here."

"Developmentally delayed," The Witch said automatically.

"Oh, sorry. I wouldn't want to say anything to hurt *them*," Brian said.

For the first time since I'd met her, The Witch looked unsure of herself. "Is that why you helped her run away?" she asked Brian. "Because we don't pay enough attention to you?"

He shook his head. "No. That was because no one else was paying attention to Rose, or helping her."

Her lips twisted with something like pride as she looked at Brian. It was a look that made me ache somehow.

Fred cleared his throat. "Rose has made a suggestion," he reminded everyone. "I'm not sure—"

"It wouldn't work for Rose to live here," The Witch said gently.

"That's right, it wouldn't," Brian said.

Ouch! Just when I think the guy has my back, he stabs me!

I tried to pull together the miniscule scraps of self-esteem I had left. "I don't suppose you want me either," I said, looking sideways at Joan. "After this, and the cops coming to your house about the computer equipment, and all that." I didn't know if the rest of the group knew about the suspected theft, but they would soon enough.

To my surprise Joan waved her hand back and forth. "Don't worry about the computer theft," she said. "Kimber went to that nice officer who has a background in foster care and told him what we suspected. They searched Mara's car and locker, and found one of the computer disks she'd forgotten to destroy."

"So they caught her?"

"Arrested her, to be exact." Joan grinned.

I felt a little victory surge too, but I tried not to show it. Instead I shot a look at Brian, wondering if he was upset about his girlfriend betraying him. But his expression was hard to read.

Joan squeezed my shoulder. "You can stay with us, Rose," she said. "I know I'm too touchy-feely for you, and that it's probably not forever. But I've loved having you in our family."

Tears welled up in my eyes. "Thanks," I said, and then got out of my chair to hug her from behind. "Thanks for everything."

Fred broke in. "I'd like for us to set a couple of goals at this meeting," he said. "The official hearing will go better if we have a plan."

A plan, a plan . . . I slid back into my seat and drummed my fingers on the table, thinking. I'd made plan after plan to get us back together, and all of them had flopped. But I knew from the fairy tales I loved that you had to keep trying, that the one who persevered was the one who got the prize, that the glass slipper fit the very last foot in the kingdom.

"I think what happened yesterday speaks to the need for some court-supervised visits between Rose, Dani, and their mother," Fred said.

The Witch sat up straighter. "But not after—"

Fred interrupted her interruption. "Court-supervised, because we don't want any more escape attempts. Visits, because it's clear this family wants to be together."

"And Mom's making progress," I blurted out. "She can leave the house. She's starting to make some plans."

Fred nodded. "Not the best of plans, yet, but you're right."

I knew I must be thinking about this all wrong, that I had to turn it around to solve the riddle.

And then it hit me. I'd been so focused on

Dani and me, and so certain our family belonged in the city, that I hadn't considered the easiest choice of all.

Well, sort of easy. And sort of incredibly hard, too. "What if Mom and I got an apartment together, here in Linden Falls?"

Everyone stared at me, and heads started shaking back and forth. The old automatic "no."

"Not this week or anything," I said, "but Mom's starting a job training program. Aren't there jobs in Linden Falls?"

"Well, actually," Fred said, "there are openings here."

Everyone took drinks of coffee at once.

After they'd clinked their cups and saucers for a while, heads started cocking and faces brightened.

"It could happen," Fred said.

"A lot depends on the court," The Witch said slowly, "but it's a reasonable goal."

"But Rose," Joan said, "do you really want to live with your mom again?"

I let that question settle inside me, trying the idea on. Me and Mom living together . . . here. Could it work?

In a way, I felt like I barely knew my own mother. We'd hardly talked in the past few years, and when we did, it was always about Dani. And I was realizing how mad I was about all those years of silent darkness.

All the same, she was my mom, and I loved her.

"You could stay with us until your mom's ready," Joan offered. "And visit afterwards. A lot."

I bit my lip. "What about Dani?"

Everyone got real quiet.

Finally Fred spoke. "That's the merit of you and your Mom being here in Linden Falls," he said. "You could see Dani, but . . . I don't think your mom will be ready to take on Dani's care any time soon."

I opened my mouth in automatic protest, and then shut it. Fred was right, and I knew it. What was more, I couldn't fool myself any longer that I, a fifteen-year-old girl, could take full-time care of an eight-year-old with Dani's problems.

"She can stay with us," The Witch said, "but as a foster child. There wouldn't be a question of our adopting her. And you and your mother could see her regularly."

"We could?" I asked. "Like, real visits where we take her out? Or have her come to our place?"

"In time," Fred said.

"I've been a little too strict about that," The Witch admitted.

And then she actually smiled at me!

Everyone seemed to be looking at me, like I was the big decision-maker. *That* felt weird. "Okay," I said. It felt a little bit like giving up, acknowledging I needed all these people to help me keep my family together in any kind of way.

But looking around at all of them made me feel stronger, too.

After that, the adults dug into the details: paperwork and courts and incident reports. Brian caught my eye and gestured toward the back door, and I limped out after him into the warm spring morning.

I was a little bit mad at him and hurt that he hadn't argued with his mom to take me in. But even so, I had to admire the way his arms bulged in his short-sleeved golf shirt.

Now I knew that he got those muscles from helping to carry the younger kids around. That made him even better looking to me.

We sat down on the back step. Sunshine warmed my face. I heard birds chirping and a couple of kids laughing and shouting out by the backyard tire swing. A rich muddy smell hung in the air.

"You know why I didn't want you to come live with us?" Brian asked.

"Because you're not my handsome prince." I pretended to pout, ready to make a joke of it.

"No," he said, putting his arm around me. "It's because I don't think of you as a sister."

"Oh, really?" I turned a little toward him but, suddenly shy, didn't meet his eyes.

"I think of you as something more."

"What about Mara?"

He brushed my hair back from my face. "That was over the first time I kissed you."

The memory of that sweet kiss gave me courage. "You make me pretty crazy sometimes," I said, "but I do like you."

"I like you too," he said, and leaned toward me.

Behind us, there was a squealing at the open screen door. "Why you kissing my Rose?" Dani asked in her usual loud voice.

Brian lifted his face but kept his arms around me. "One problem with being my girlfriend," he said, "is that you'll end up spending a lot of time around here. We don't get a whole lot of privacy."

I reached back to open the door so Dani could come out.

She flopped down in both our laps. "Hug me too," she ordered.

I hugged her tight while Brian tickled her bare feet until we sprawled like a heap of giggling little kids on the ground.

"What's going on out there?" The Witch called.

"Nothing, Mom," Brian yelled back.

"What you said, about the privacy problem." I lounged against Brian's delicious shoulders. "I'm okay with it."